Bloomability

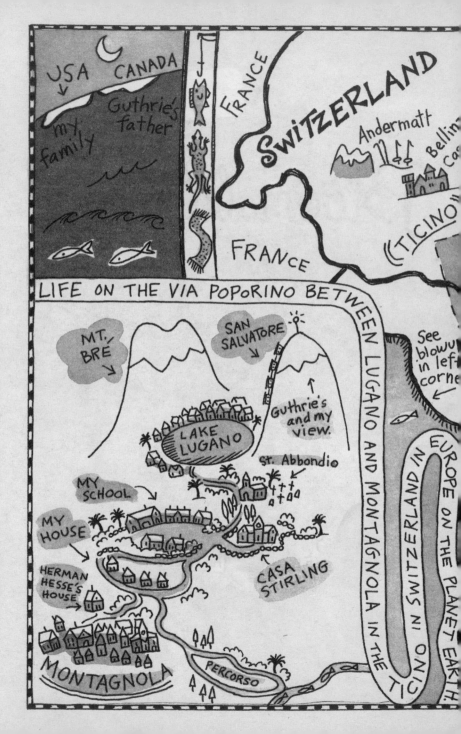

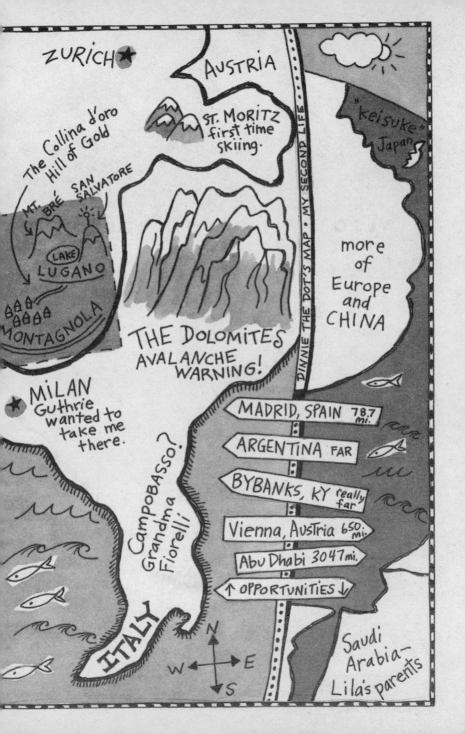

ALSO BY SHARON CREECH

Walk Two Moons

Chasing Redbird

SHARON CREECH

Bloomability

SCHOLASTIC INC.

New York Toronto London Auckland Sydney
Mexico City New Delhi Hong Kong

ISBN 0-439-10476-9

12 11 10 9 8 7   1 2 3 4/0

Printed in the U.S.A.   40

First Scholastic printing, September 1999

Map illustration by Holly Berry
Typography by Alicia Mikles

For
Anna Maria Licursi Creech
and
Mary Crist Fleming

With thanks to
Melissa Maier
for refreshing my Italian.

∾ Contents ∾

I become a transparent eyeball . . .
—Ralph Waldo Emerson,
Nature

1

◡: First Life :◡

In my first life, I lived with my mother, and my older brother and sister, Crick and Stella, and with my father when he wasn't on the road. My father was a trucker, or sometimes a mechanic or a picker, a plucker or painter. He called himself a Jack-of-all-trades (Jack was his real name), but sometimes there wasn't any trade in whatever town we were living in, so off he would go in search of a job somewhere else. My mother would start packing, and we'd wait for a phone call from him that would tell us it was time to join him.

He'd always say, "I found us a great place! Wait'll you see it!"

Each time we moved, we had fewer boxes, not more. My mother would say, "Do you really need all those *things*, Dinnie? They're just *things*. Leave them."

By the time I was twelve, we'd followed my father from Kentucky to Virginia to North Carolina to Tennessee to Ohio to Indiana to Wisconsin to Oklahoma to Oregon to Texas to California to New Mexico. My things fit in one box. Sometimes we lived in the middle of a noisy city, but most of the time Dad had found us a tilted house on a forgotten road near a forgotten town.

My mother had been a city girl, my father a country boy; and as far as I could tell, my mother spent most of her time trying to forget that she'd been a city girl. Those few times that we lived in the middle of the city, though, she seemed as if she were right at home, in her real home, her permanent home. She'd get a job in an office or a design studio, instead of a diner. She knew how to use buses and weave in and out of crowds, and she didn't seem to hear the horns and sirens and jackhammers.

Those things drove my father crazy. "I *know* there's work here," he'd say, "but there's too many bodies and cars everywhere. You're like to get killed just stepping into the road. No place to raise kids."

My mother would be real quiet after he'd said something like this, and pretty soon he'd be off looking for a better place to live, and she'd be packing again. My sister Stella had a theory that Dad was keeping us on the move so my mother's family wouldn't find us. He didn't trust a single one of her brothers or sisters, and he didn't trust her parents, either. He thought they had "airs" and would talk my mother into moving back to New York, where she'd come from. He said they looked down their noses at us.

Once, when I was seven or eight, and we were living in Wisconsin—or no, maybe it was Oklahoma—or it could've been Arkansas (I forgot Arkansas—we lived there for six months, I believe), a thin woman with gray hair pulled back in a tight bun was sitting in our kitchen one day when I came home from school. Before I could shake off my coat, she'd wrapped me in a perfumed hug and called me *carissima* and her *sweet kitten*.

"I'm not a kitten," I said, sliding out the side door. Crick was throwing a basketball at an invisible hoop.

"There's a lady in there," I said.

Crick aimed, shot that ball into a graceful high arc, and watched it bounce off the edge of the garage next door. "Crud," he said, "that's no lady. That's your grandma Fiorelli."

There was a big argument that night after I'd gone to bed behind the drapes hung between the kitchen and the side room. My Dad was gone— he'd taken one look at our lady grandma and bolted out the door, never even pausing to say hello. It was Mom and Grandma in the kitchen.

Mom was telling her how resourceful Dad was, and how he could do anything, and what a rich life we had. From the bed next to mine, Stella said, "Mom's a dreamer."

In the kitchen, Grandma said, "Rich? This is a rich life?"

My mother charged on. "Money isn't everything, Ma," she said.

"And why you go and let him name that boy *Crick*? What kind of name is that? Sounds like he was raised in a barn."

My parents had had an agreement. Dad got to name any boys they had, and Mom got to name the girls. Dad told me he'd named Crick after a clear little crick that ran beside the house they'd lived in at the time. Once, when I used the word *crick* in a paper for school, the teacher crossed it out and wrote *creek* above it. She said *crick* wasn't a real word. I didn't tell Dad that. Or Crick either.

Mom named her first girl (my sister) Stella Maria. Then I came along, and she must have been saving up for me, because she named me Domenica Santolina Doone. My name means Sunday-Southern-Wood-River. I was born on a Sunday (which makes me blessed, Mom said), and at the time we lived in the South beside woods and a river. My name is pronounced in the Italian way: Doe-MEN-i-kuh. Domenica Santolina Doone. It's a mouthful, so most people call me Dinnie.

In the kitchen, Grandma Fiorelli was steaming on. "You ought to think of yourself," she said. "You ought to think of those children. They could be in a school like the one your sister works in. Your husband needs a real job——"

"He has a real job——"

"Every six months? *Basta!*" Grandma said. "Why he can't keep a job for more than six months at a time? What does he do, anyway? Why he didn't go to college so he could get a real job? How are you going to get out of this mess?"

"He's looking for the right opportunity," my mother said. "He could do anything—anything at all. He just needs a break—"

Grandma's voice got louder every time she started up again. She was bellowing like a bull by this time. "A break? *É ridicolo!* And how he is going to get a break if he doesn't even have a college education? Answer me that!"

"Everybody doesn't need a college education," my mother said.

"When we come to this country, your father and I, we know not a word of English, but you kids got a college education—"

Stella threw a pillow at me. "Don't listen, Dinnie," she said. "Put your head under this and go to sleep."

The pillow didn't drown out Grandma Fiorelli, though. She barreled on. "And what about you?" Grandma said to my mother. "There you are, a perfectly well-trained artist, and I bet you don't even have a paintbrush to your name."

"I paint," my mother said.

"Like what? Walls? Falling down, peeling walls? *Basta!* You ought to talk to your sister—"

The next morning Grandma Fiorelli was gone, and so was Dad. He'd gone looking for a new place to live. He'd heard of an opportunity, he said.

And so we followed him around, from opportunity to opportunity, and as we went, Crick got into more and more trouble. Crick said it wasn't his fault that every place we went, he met up with people who made him do bad things. According to Crick, some boys in Oklahoma made him throw rocks at the school windows, and some boys in Oregon made him slash a tire, and some boys in Texas made him smoke a joint, and some boys in California made him burn down a barn, and some boys in New Mexico made him steal a car.

Every time we moved, Dad told him, "You can start over."

And with each move, Stella got quieter and quieter. Within a week of our reaching a new town, there'd be boys pounding on the door day and night, wanting to see her. All kinds of boys: tough ones, quiet ones, nerdy ones, cool ones.

In California, when she was sixteen, she came

home one Sunday night, after having been gone all weekend with one of her girlfriends, supposedly, and said she'd gotten married.

"No you didn't," Dad said.

"Okay, I didn't," she said, and went on up to bed.

She told me she'd married a Marine, and she showed me a marriage certificate. The Marine was going overseas. Stella started eating and eating and eating. She got rounder and rounder and rounder. When we were in that hill town in New Mexico, she woke me up one night and said, "Get Mom, and get her quick."

Stella was having a baby. Dad was on the road, Crick was in jail, and Stella was having a baby.

And that was the last week of my first life.

2

∾: The Dot :∾

The Dreams of Domenica Santolina Doone

My mother bundled me up in a brown cardboard box and taped it all around and gave it to the strangers. I rumbled along and then I was in the bottom of an airplane next to another box which barked. There was a dog biscuit in the bottom of my box, and when I got hungry, I ate it.

My second life began when I was kidnapped by two complete strangers. My mother, who assisted in this kidnapping, said I was exaggerating. The strangers weren't complete strangers. I'd met them twice before. They were my mother's sister and her husband: Aunt Sandy and Uncle Max. They swooped down on our little New Mexico hill town and stayed up all night talking to my mother. In the morning, we all went to see Stella and her new baby boy, and then my aunt and uncle forced me into their car (okay, they didn't completely *force* me, but no one asked my opinion about this kidnapping). With me was my box of things, and we drove to the airport in Albuquerque.

I was still pretty much in bubble mode. It seemed that all around me was a smooth bubble, clear enough to see through, but strong enough to keep me inside. It was like a huge transparent beach ball. I imagined pores in this bubble ball that could let in streams of things from the outside, so I could examine them and poke them back out again if I didn't like them. On the car trip to Albuquerque, the pores were closed, sealed off. When I got to the airport, though, I couldn't help it, a few of those pores opened up on their own. Defiant pores.

I'd never been on a plane. Uncle Max gave my box of things to a woman in a uniform. Aunt Sandy bought me M&M's and an illustrated book of fairy tales. I was much too old for fairy tales, and told her so, but she said, "I'll let you in on a secret. *I* read them all the time, and I'm ancient!"

We sat in a room, and then we got in a line and walked down a tunnel and sat in narrow seats, and this was the airplane. When the plane started speeding down the runway, I closed up my bubble tight, ready for the crash. I knew that plane wasn't going to go up in the air like it was supposed to. I bent over and held my knees in crash position, which is what a little card in the seat pocket told you to do. Aunt Sandy patted my back.

"We're gonna die!" I said. The noise was awful, a huge bellowing whooshing and roaring, and all the time Aunt Sandy patted my back as if she didn't care if she got all smooshed up in the crash or not. Then the front of the plane pointed up and the whole thing, people and all, lifted up and we were flying.

Flying! My nose was against the window the whole way, all across the country. I was up in the sky and we went right through clouds and sometimes we could see puffy white blankets of clouds below us, and sometimes there were no clouds and we could see mountains and rivers and lakes and roads. In one blink, there were whole towns and then, zip, they were gone, and there was a desert and more mountains and hills and flat land. There was green land and brown land. It was a miracle.

It wasn't anything like driving, where you only see this little bit and that little bit: a house, a tree, a gas station, more houses, more trees, fields. In a car it all starts to run together and you could be anywhere or nowhere. In the plane, you saw it all spread out beneath you, a living map, a wide, wide living photograph, and you were suspended above it and you knew where you were. You were a dot, miles and miles and miles above the state of Oklahoma where you had once lived on a speck of dirt, and you were a dot above the state of Arkansas where you'd even forgotten you'd lived, and you were a dot above Tennessee and Virginia. You little dot.

Or rather *me*: Dinnie the dot.

The plane came down again without crashing and we went to Aunt Sandy and Uncle Max's house in Washington, D. C., where there were two bathrooms that worked, and there was clean car-pet and white walls with paintings in frames. My father, who'd been away on an opportunity when

I'd been kidnapped, called and cried on the phone and wished me luck in my opportunity.

I didn't like to hear him cry and I didn't want an opportunity, but Aunt Sandy and Uncle Max seemed very excited, and so I felt I should do what they told me to do until I could plan my escape. I felt as if this were happening to someone else. It was happening to that Domenica Santolina Doone person, but I was Dinnie in my bubble, and I was just watching, planning Domenica's escape.

The next day, that Domenica Santolina Doone person got her picture taken and applied for a passport, and two weeks later, we were in an airport again. This time we flew into the night and over the ocean, and in the middle of the night, suspended over the ocean, the sun came up, zip, and it was morning before the night was over, and we ate real food, not dog biscuits. The plane swooped over jagged snow-covered mountains and landed without crashing in Zurich, Switzerland. A foreign country.

Uncle Max was going to be the new headmaster at a school in Lugano, in the south of

Switzerland, and Aunt Sandy was going to teach there, and Domenica Santolina Doone was going to live with them and go to their school. Domenica Santolina Doone in Switzerland. It was an opportunity.

3

∽: An Opportunity :∼

In the train station in Zurich, people rushed this way, that way, a herd of confused animals. Trains lined up side by side like a row of cattle cars, and people climbed in, climbed out. We stood under the departure board.

"Platform four," Aunt Sandy said. She looked like my mother, but she was all dressed up in clothes that matched. She sounded like my mother, too, but her words came out faster than my mother's words did. "Way down there, at the end—run!"

"You're sure?" Uncle Max said. He was very tall, with black curly hair and didn't look at all like my father. He looked like someone in an advertisement, clean and neat, even after our long flight. I was wearing the remains of my dinner on my shirt.

"That's the one?" Uncle Max said. "It stops in Lugano?"

Aunt Sandy waved at the board which listed the stops. "Right there—see? Zug—Arth Goldau—Bellinzona—Lugano—"

Uncle Max hurried down the gray platform, pushing a cart with their suitcases and my box on it. "Dinnie?" he called behind him. "Don't lose us—"

They'd bought me new clothes and new black shoes which hurt my feet, but I pretended that the shoes didn't hurt, because they were new and they'd cost a lot of money. These shoes had a mind of their own. They kept clunking into each other, making me trip, and I had to stare down at them and order them to point in the right direction. I felt as if I were trying to keep two little kids from squabbling with each other.

All around us people rushed, calling to each other in German and French and Italian. Mostly it sounded like *achtenspit flickenspit* and *ness-pa siss-pah* and *mumble-mumble-ino giantino mumble-ino.* And then I realized that I recognized some of the Italian words—*Ciao! Arrividerci! Andiamo!* My mother said these words sometimes. I wanted to stop, to listen to what everybody was saying. It was as if they were speaking in code, and I needed to wait and get all the clues. Maybe they were saying, *Fire! Fire!* or *Run for your lives!*

"Dinnie!" Aunt Sandy called. "Hurry!"

I didn't have to go. I could fade into the crowd, be pushed along through the tunnel, into the city. I could roll along in my bubble ball.

I was used to moving, used to packing up and following along like a robot, but I was tired of it. I wanted to stop moving and I wanted to be somewhere and stay somewhere and I wanted my family.

In New Mexico, I'd heard my mother tell Aunt Sandy, "Dinnie will be fine, just fine. She's very adaptable."

As I stood there in that busy Zurich train station, I was sorry I was so adaptable, and I promised myself that I was going to stop being adaptable.

It's hard to change your character overnight, though.

"Dinnie! Dinnie!" Aunt Sandy called.

A small brown bird darted back and forth under the domed ceiling. At the far end of the station, near the high ceiling, was an open window.

There, I urged the bird, *over there.*

"Dinnie!"

Uncle Max heaved the luggage up onto the train and Aunt Sandy, now standing in the carriage, pulled it into the aisle. I—little adaptable robot Dinnie—followed Uncle Max aboard and the stationmaster closed the door behind us. A whistle blew.

The clock on the platform clicked as the train slipped away from the station, and I slid into a seat opposite my aunt and uncle.

"Oh, Dinnie!" Aunt Sandy said. "We made it!" She pressed her face to the window. "Look at it, look! Oh, Switzerland!"

Click, click, whoosh. The train rushed out of the city, around the edge of the lake, through a deep green valley, and then up, up, up into the mountains. Through dark tunnels. Up, up, up, crisscrossing the mountain, and down, down, down. *Whishhhhh.*

"Oh, I can hardly stand it!" Aunt Sandy said. "Look at this—"

Uncle Max pressed his hand against hers. Steep stone cliffs and high green pastures whizzed past as the train curved through the mountains. Gushing waterfalls came into view and then vanished. Clear rivers raced beside the train, looping and curving alongside the tracks. Little houses looked as if they were stuck into the side of mountains, planted there, blooming up out of the ground. Aunt Sandy called these little houses *chalets*. *Chalets*—it was a smooth word. I said it over and over in my mind: *chalets, chalets, chalets*. It made me sleepy.

. . . .

The Dreams of Domenica Santolina Doone

I was in a box, swaying from side to side. The box was labeled ROBOT and was on wheels and it rushed down tracks which turned into a dinosaur's spine and then into a river.

. . . .

Through the Alps the train rushed, as if on a mission, urgent and efficient. Maybe they were really taking me to a prison, where I'd be chained up and fed moldy bread and brown water.

I started wondering if I could get used to moldy bread. I could even see myself nibbling at it, trying to keep my strength up. A nibble of bread, a sip of brown water. I could adjust to that. Then I thought, *No! I won't adjust! I won't adapt! I won't! I'll rebel!*

On the train, we passed a man and two children fishing in a mountain stream, and I had a rolling pang of homesickness. My father had taught me how to fish and often we'd sit on riverbanks, casting our lines into the water, sitting there quietly, hardly ever saying a word. He loved being outside. You could just see it on his face, a big grin as soon as we'd head off, a wider one when we reached the river, and loud sighs as we'd sit there staring at the stream.

When we'd get home, my mother would always say, "Catch anything?" Sometimes we had caught a few fish, but mostly we hadn't, and at those times, my father would say, "Caught the sun! Caught the day!"

My mother loved that; she loved it to pieces. She'd kiss his cheek and say, "You are a prince among men."

In the train rolling through Switzerland, I slept

and woke, slept and woke, as it all raced by. Three hours later, the train rolled through gentler valleys and pulled into a hillside platform.

"Lu-gan-o!" the announcer called. "Lu-gan-o!"

We were deep in the foothills of the Alps, Uncle Max said, in the southern base of Switzerland. We stepped out on the platform. Across the street, and down below, the city of Lugano curled around a lake. Two mountains towered over the city, and their shadows fell across the water. The mountains stood dark against the sky, like giant guards. No sign of a prison yet.

We climbed into a taxi, which wound its way out of Lugano and up a rolling hill between the mountains and onto the Collina d'Oro, which meant *the hill of gold*, Uncle Max said, but it wasn't gold. The hill was green and brown, the road was gray. Around the narrow bends the taxi raced until Uncle Max called—"There! That's it!"

Near the road was a sign and off to the left, tucked in a rim of trees, stood an old red-roofed villa. From the outside, the villa looked dignified and sturdy and vast and frightening. Pale stone walls, iron balconies, tall black-rimmed windows.

It looked like a picture in the book Sandy and Max had given me. In the book, a princess was locked in a tower of the villa.

Inside were dark wooden floors and dim, narrow hallways. Doors and shutters creaked and groaned. Dusty portraits lined the halls: grim-faced men in black robes stared directly, accusingly, at me, and some faced sideways, ignoring me. In the dining hall ancient armor and weapons splattered the walls: shields and spears and helmets, ghastly dark shapes. I listened for sounds of captive princesses.

This is the place that Mrs. Stirling had chosen to set up an American school for students from all over the world. This is the place where I'd go to school. I wouldn't be alone, like the boarding students would be, Uncle Max said. I'd be living with him and Aunt Sandy.

I still thought they might be luring me to a prison, and I still didn't understand why I was here, why I couldn't be with my mother and father and Crick and Stella and the new baby. I thought it was because I'd done something wrong, and this was my punishment. Or maybe they had to make room for the new baby and one of us had to go. Me.

We crossed a courtyard and climbed a hill. "We'll get the luggage later," Uncle Max said. "I should have had the taxi drop us at the top of the hill." We climbed steep stone steps, winding through trees—some with strange orange fruit and others with yellow flowers that smelled sweet, like jam. We reached the Via Poporino, a narrow paved lane, and passed a yellow house, a gray one, a pink one, and then stopped in front of a white one with a red roof. A chalet.

"Oh, Max!" Aunt Sandy cried. "I am in paradise!"

Uncle Max fished the keys from his pocket. It was cool and dark in the narrow entryway. Red tiled floors. White stucco walls.

"We have gone to heaven!" Aunt Sandy said. "Look at this—"

We followed her into a wide open room with a high beamed ceiling. The far wall was a bank of windows and glass doors. We followed her through the glass doors and out onto the balcony. "Have you ever in your whole life—?" she said. "Have you ever seen—?"

Across the valley was the lake. That evening, pale lights shone all the way down the hillside and crisscrossed the mountain opposite, like a string of Christmas lights. A single red light blinked at the top.

"The valley," Aunt Sandy said, "the lake, the mountains—"

"What do you think, Dinnie?" Uncle Max asked. "Isn't it great? Don't you think it's great?"

I thought about the hilltop village in New Mexico and I thought about Stella's new baby coming home. It would all be new to him. I stared across at the mountain, huge and dark and vast.

"Sure," I said. "It's great."

But I didn't mean it. Later I would be able to look at this view and to see it and appreciate it, and it would affect me profoundly. But on that first day, I could only see what wasn't there: my family.

4

◦: The Two Prisoners :◦

. . . .

The Dreams of Domenica Santolina Doone

I was holding Stella's baby on the balcony. The baby cried and cried. On the mountain opposite, my father was looking through binoculars. I waved and called to him, but he didn't see me or hear me.

. . . .

I had walked up the Collina d'Oro to the village of Montagnola and was coming down the back way, on a path that led from the village at the top of the hill and wound down past the headmaster's house. It was Aunt Sandy and Uncle Max's house now, and they called it their *casa*.

"Not a chalet?" I'd asked.

"Well, it is a chalet. That's the style," Aunt Sandy said. "But the Italian word for house is *casa*, so this is our *casa*." They'd been trying to teach me bits of Italian because that's what the local people spoke.

"Your *chalet casa?*" I said.

"Ours," she said. "Our *chalet casa.*"

I was all mixed up about where I was. Uncle Max had told me we were in the Ticino, and in the Ticino people spoke Italian. In other parts of Switzerland, he said, people spoke German or French or Romansh.

"I thought we were in Lugano," I said.

"Lugano's down there," he said, pointing to the city below. "And the village of Montagnola's up there behind us."

"So where are *we?*" I asked.

He shrugged. "In a casa on the Via Poporino between Lugano and Montagnola in the Ticino in Switzerland in Europe on the planet Earth."

"Oh," I said.

I put up a sign in my bedroom window that said, KIDNAPPED! HELD AGAINST MY WILL! but Aunt Sandy said, "People might not be able to read it in English." She bought me an English-Italian dictionary.

On my way down the path from Montagnola,

I was thinking about the two prisoners. It was a story that a boy, Guthrie, had told me the day before: There were two prisoners in a jail cell. They each looked out the same small window. One prisoner said, "Man oh man, what a lot of dirt!" The other said, "Man oh man, what a lot of sky!"

"That's it?" I had said when Guthrie finished. "That's all there is to the story?"

"Think about it," Guthrie said.

So I'd been thinking and thinking about it. Beneath my feet was a crumbling stone path, splattered with rotting persimmons. Pieces of the orange fruit were stuck to my new shoes. Wasps dived in and out of the fruit, and a lizard darted along the edge of an old stone wall. What did the lizard see? Could he see only the path and rotting persimmons and wasps?

Then I looked up, like the second prisoner must have done. Ahead were palm trees lining the path, a blue sky with puffs of white clouds, and hills rolling toward the blue lake. Switzerland curled along one shore, and Italy sprawled on the other.

Mountains ringed most of the lake, with the two taller ones standing on opposite shores. On top of Mt. San Salvatore, the red light blinked, and on top of Mt. Bré was a ragged peak dipping into a shallow bowl. Guthrie had said that by October there would be snow on the top of Mt. Bré.

This seemed weird, that I could be standing in Switzerland and see Italy, and it was weird that palm trees and snow could be in the same scene. And it seemed weird that I was in that scene.

If I closed my eyes, maybe I'd feel as if I were in New Mexico. It didn't smell the same as New Mexico, and the air didn't feel the same, but still, if I kept my eyes closed long enough, maybe I could change it to New Mexico. Then I could look in the windows of our house and see my mother and father and Stella and the new baby. If they saw me, though, they might be mad that I'd come back.

When a persimmon fell on my head, interrupting my dream, I yelled at it and at the tree overhead and at the wasp that zoomed in on my hair. "Hey!" The lizard skittered up the wall, as if he knew where he was going. He had a mission. Could he see sky? Did I have a mission? If I were in prison and looked out the window, would I see dirt or sky?

I didn't understand what I was supposed to see. It seemed like part of Guthrie's story about the prisoners was missing.

There was still a week before school opened. Guthrie had said he was dropping off his luggage and then going on to stay with friends in Milan until then. It would be Guthrie's second year at the school. I thought he was older than I was, but he said he was thirteen, just like me. "You're going by yourself to Milan?" I had asked.

"It's not far—heck, you can probably see it from the top of San Salvatore! *Milano!*" He kissed his fingers, and raised his hand to the sky, a gesture that seemed odd, foreign, and that made him seem worldy. I copied the gesture, and he smiled.

"How do you get there?" I asked.

"You just get on the train and off you go— *presto!* There in no time! You should try it. Come with me if you want—"

Guthrie might as well have suggested that I pack up and make my way to Africa. I was having enough trouble dealing with the small patch of Switzerland on which I'd been planted.

In the week since I'd arrived, I'd explored the areas around Max and Sandy's house, in small chunks. I circled the campus on the first day. On the second, I walked the length of the Via Poporino, and today I'd gone all the way up the Collina d'Oro to the village of Montagnola and was coming home the back way, along the path. Tomorrow I was going down the hill, to the church of St. Abbondio. I was like a cat, scoping out my territory. This was something I did automatically, every place I lived.

Guthrie had asked where I was going until school started. "Nowhere," I said. "I have to live here—with the new—with my uncle." I didn't want to say I lived with the headmaster.

"*Have* to live here?" Guthrie said. "I'd give my right arm to live here, all the time, all the whole year round."

"Well, I wouldn't," I said.

And that's when Guthrie had told me about the two prisoners.

• • •

When I got home that day, Aunt Sandy showed me a spider plant that a neighbor had given her. It had slender pale green and white leaves, stretching upward, and dozens of offshoots, which Aunt Sandy said were its children. The children had little roots dangling from them, in the air, as if they were reaching for the soil. That was me, I thought, a little plant with my roots dangling in the air.

That night I looked up *kidnapped* in my new dictionary. There were several choices, and I chose *portare via a forza* and made a new sign.

Aunt Sandy said, "I think that what you've written means *take by force*, like a command, as if you are asking someone to come into the house and kidnap you. Is that what you wanted to say?"

No, I did not. But neither of us could figure out how to change *take by force* to *taken by force*.

Next I tried *Help!* but there were so many choices for that one word that I finally just aimed my pencil and stabbed at one. *SERVITEVI!* I wrote.

When Uncle Max came in to say good night,

he looked at my sign and said, "I think that what you've written means *Help yourself!* You know, as if you are inviting the burglars in to take all our belongings. Is that what you meant?"

5

⌁ Postcards ⌁

My father has two sisters, Grace and Tillie. They still live in Bybanks, Kentucky, the town in which both my father and I were born. Grace and Tillie were always big on writing postcards and letters, keeping us filled in on their news, but still I was surprised to receive a postcard from Aunt Grace just a few weeks after I arrived in Switzerland.

> *Dear Dinnie,*
>
> *I hope you arrived at Switzerland okay and did not have any hijackers on your plane. I would of prayed for you but I didn't even know you were going until after you'd gone.*
>
> *How is it there? Do you need to speak Switz or what? Have you been fishing yet? Do you have different food? I made pot roast for tonight. It's Lonnie's favorite.*
>
> *Tillie's coming over any second and bringing some*

of that awful cheesecake jello she makes, and I got to
pretend I like it.

    I am sending you a bushel of hugs,
    Love, love, love,
    Your Aunt Grace

    The next day this postcard came from Grace's
sister Tillie:

Dear Dinnie,

    *I had a call from your daddy and he was just
heartbroke over you going all the way to Switzerland
but he says it is an opportunity and he hopes you have
the time of your life.*

    *I was wondering if you have to wear those leather
shorts and kneesocks or is that just boys? Are you still
fishing?*

    *I've got to go over to Grace's for dinner. I'm
taking her my cheesecake jello which won a prize, did
you know that? Grace is having pot roast which don't
usually turn out too good, but she tries.*

    Here are a thousand kisses for you:

    xxxxxxxxxxxxxxxxxxxxxxxxxx

xxxxxxxxxxxxxxxxxxxxxxxxxxxxxxx

xxxxxxxxxxxxxxxxxxxxxxxxxxxxx
xxxxxxxxxxxxxxxxxxxxxxxxxxxxx
xxxxxxxxxxxxxxxxxxxxxxxxxxxxx
xxxxxxxxxxxxxxxxxxxxxxxx.

Love from your Aunt Tillie

What I didn't receive was mail from my parents. They'd forgotten me.

I wasn't all that surprised that they could forget me. Once, when we were driving from Oklahoma to Oregon, or maybe it was from Oregon to Texas, we stopped at a rest stop, and when I came out of the bathroom, the car was gone.

In the parking lot, a couple and their three children were climbing back into their camper. I wondered if they'd take me with them. If we couldn't find my parents, maybe they would let me live with them.

But I wasn't brave enough to ask, and so I sat on a picnic table and watched cars and campers come and go, come and go, and I was just nodding off to sleep when I heard Crick calling, "Dinnie! Dinnie!" and there they all were, piling out of the car and ruffling my hair and my mother was crying and my father was laughing and Stella said, "Dinnie! Don't you ever do that again! You scared us half to death!"

For the rest of the trip, I did not get out of the car, even to go to the bathroom or to eat.

6

~: The Girl :~

The air was hot and thick, the way it had been sometimes in Texas and Oklahoma, and clouds hung over the valley as I ran down the Collina d'Oro. Just past the far edge of the school campus, the road zipped left, dipped past a clump of old stone buildings, and zipped right. Then I could see the church spread below, and beyond that the hill dipped to the lake. Across from the church was Mt. San Salvatore.

It was odd how the mountain seemed to loom there. From my bedroom window, it seemed that the mountain faced me, the house. But from this different angle, there it was again, the mountain, but now it faced the church.

Boom! Boom-boom-boom! That morning, I'd been standing on the balcony at Uncle Max's when I'd first heard the sound. *Boom!* A loud, dull thundering, followed by its echoes through the valley.

I'd rushed inside. "We're being bombed! We're going to die!"

Uncle Max followed me out to the balcony. Soon there was another *Boom! Boom-boom-boom!*

"We're going to die!"

"Dinnie—" He placed his hand on my arm. "It's not a bomb. It's military practice. They do it every weekend." He said he'd reacted much the same as I had when he first visited the school a year ago.

"You did?" I said.

"Well, I didn't think I was going to die, but yes, it did sound like bombs going off."

"But why do they have military practice? Switzerland is neutral—"

"Neutral doesn't mean you don't have to be prepared to defend yourself," Uncle Max said.

Boom! I was standing on the road near the church, listening to the continued booms in the valley. Leading up to the church was a walkway, a long, narrow path, with a double row of cypress trees lining it. The trees were tall and thin, like dark unlit candles stretching to the sky. At the end of the path sat the church, square and built of yellow stone, with a tall clock tower rising up from its center.

Midway down the path was a girl. She was wearing a white shirt and shorts, moving slowly along toward the church, as if she were being pulled toward it by an invisible rope. By the time I reached the path, she had entered the church. The only sound was the distant hum of cars along the *autostrada* across the valley. All else was quiet. No birds, no people, nothing but that hum. It was five minutes to ten.

The church door was open. Inside it was dark except for a spot of gold light coming through a round window high on the far wall. It was cooler here, and even quieter, and I listened for sounds of the girl, but I was thinking of Stella and Crick and my parents and the new baby, listening for them, too.

I stood at the back until my eyes adjusted to the darkness. Gradually, I made out the row of dark pews, the center aisle, and then I saw her, sitting at the far end of a pew. Her hands were folded in her lap and her head was tilted up toward the window with the golden light. I imagined that it was Stella sitting there, and we weren't in Switzerland at all. We were in America.

I went back outside and leaned against the cool wall. Just as the girl came through the door, the bells began tolling the hour. "Oh!" she said, startled. She looked at me and up at the tower where the bells were swinging. "*Listen* to that! It sounds so—so—"

"Weird?" I said.

"No, not *weird!*" she said. "Amazing—and incredible—and—" She stepped toward me. "Are you American? I'm American!"

"Me, too," I said. I hoped she wasn't going to ask me where I was from. That was always a hard question to answer. Did people mean originally or most recently or what?

"Are you going to the American school here? I am," she said.

"I guess I am."

She squinted at me. "You *guess*? Don't you know?"

I'd been thinking that I was going to escape before school started, or that my parents might

come and rescue me, but what I said to her was,
"My uncle's the headmaster, so yep, I'll be going
to the school."

"How exciting!" she said. "I'm going to start
fresh here!"

I wondered what she meant by that and
thought she might explain, but instead she chattered on about other things, telling me that she
was staying with her parents in a hotel up in
Montagnola and that they were going off traveling for a few days and then she'd be back for the
opening of school, and then her parents were
returning to Saudi Arabia, where her father was
working. "I'm Lila," she added. "Who are you?"

Her name had a nice sound: *Li-la*.

"Me?" I said. "I'm Dinnie."

"That's a funny name," she said, but before
I could be insulted, she grabbed my arm. "Come
on," she said, "we'll walk down to Lugano!" Just
beyond the church, in the next village, she phoned
her parents. I heard her say, "She says she's the
headmaster's niece. I'm sure she's *safe*, Mom."

On the way down to Lugano, she said, "You'll
live here all year then? Imagine living here all year.

It's like—like—I don't know—like a paradise."

"Sometimes it rains," I said.

She laughed—a laugh that began way back in her throat as a soft bubbling, and then it rolled and curled out of her mouth and into the air until it wrapped the trees and bushes. I would have laughed with her, but I was sure that my own laugh would sound inferior in comparison.

I asked her if she'd met any other students yet. "Only one," Lila said. "The other day—a boy. Guthrie, that was his name. You know what he did? He invited me to go to Milan with him. Milan! What a crazy guy. As if my parents would let me trundle off to Milan with some stranger! He seemed nice, though, you know?"

So Guthrie had invited each of us to Milan. I'd only just met him, and I knew nothing about him, but I was disappointed that he hadn't invited just me. I would have confided this to Lila, but I'd learned the hard way that you shouldn't confess too much to people you've just met. On my second day of school in California, I told a girl that I had a crush on one of the boys. By lunchtime, that news was all over the whole school. Two girls accosted me on my way home and told me, "You think you're special because you're the new kid? Well, let us tell you something. That guy's already spoken for, and you're nothin' special."

So, even though I was disappointed that Guthrie had also invited Lila to Milan, I didn't say so to her.

In a wide, open square in the heart of Lugano, we sat at an outdoor café and, after much pointing at the menu, ordered pizzas. Mine came with strange brown things on it.

Lila said, "Those are anchovies."

"What's that?"

"You don't know what anchovies are?" she said. "They're intsy bitsy fishes. Very salty."

I stared at them. They looked like smashed centipedes. I picked them off and hid them under a piece of crust.

"Listen," Lila said. "No one is speaking English! Isn't that neat? We could say anything, and no one would understand."

"My uncle says that most people here know English. It's just that we can't understand *them*."

"Really?" Lila said. "Well, I'm glad you told me that. I might have said something I'd regret."

But I couldn't imagine her saying anything she'd regret, or minding if she did. I liked being with her at the outdoor table, as if I had a friend, squeezed in among so many strangers.

In the center of the square, a juggler was tossing red balls. Pigeons pecked and wobbled across the pavement. On all four sides of the square, tall buildings stood. I couldn't see the mountain. It was there, I knew it, beyond the buildings, beyond the trees, but from where we sat, I couldn't see it, and I felt safe.

That mountain had seemed to stare at me, and it was so dark and big, always looming there, blocking out everything behind it. It also reminded me of mountains where I'd lived with my family, and because of that, it was a constant reminder of their absence.

I would sometimes be caught off guard, thinking about something else—maybe the bells of St. Abbondio, maybe the narrow, curving streets of Switzerland—and then I'd see the mountain and be reminded of my family, and I'd feel guilty that I hadn't been thinking of them, and that I was actually liking some things about this new place.

What if I adapted completely, what if I forgot about them, what if they forgot about me?

When we returned to Lila's hotel in Montagnola, her father was sitting on the terrace, his face turned toward the sun. Lila introduced me.

"American?" he said. "Your uncle's the headmaster? I hope he knows what he's doing." He laughed, but his laugh was not warm like Lila's; it was cold and mocking. Beyond him, a slim Crossair jet slipped through the slot of the valley, skimming low, like a slender white and red flying fish.

As I left, I turned to look at them one more time. Lila was facing her father and his finger was pointed at her, as if warning her. She patted his shoulder and laughed, and I could hear that laugh as I walked back down the hill. I heard it all the way back down the Collina d'Oro, long after it would have been possible to hear it, even if she had continued laughing.

• • •

The Dreams of Domenica Santolina Doone

I was an anchovy, floating on a cloud, and a bird flew by. The bird was laughing, laughing, laughing. It was flying toward the mountain. I wanted to say "Watch out, watch out!" but I was not a talking anchovy. And then I slipped through a hole in the cloud and fell down, down, down. I never landed. I woke up.

7

∼: The Queen :∼

Mrs. Stirling, the school's founder and owner, swept into town the day before school opened. From the way the faculty and staff were fluttering in anticipation of her visit, you'd have thought the Queen herself was arriving. And in a way, once you'd met her, you felt as if maybe you *had* met the Queen.

I don't know how old she was. She said she was a hundred and five, but she was joking. Some people guessed sixty or sixty-five or seventy. I didn't have a clue. From the way she acted, you wouldn't even think she was sixty.

She had a puff of salt-and-pepper hair and always wore low-cut black dresses, a long string of pearls, huge sparkly earrings, and spiked black heels. This was her uniform, altered only occasionally and only slightly, with the exchange, say, of spiked red heels for the spiked black ones. She was very elegant-looking, and when she glided into a room, everyone turned to look at her. Mrs. Stirling knew nearly everyone's name and spoke fluent English, French, and Italian, and she could switch from one language to another in the blink of an eye.

Her house, Casa Stirling, a rambling four-hundred-year-old stone building with a tall bell tower, sat on the edge of campus. She also had homes on the campuses of her other schools in France and Spain and England, and she had a villa in Italy, and she spent her life dashing from one school or home to the other, usually spending a week at a time at each.

Mrs. Stirling drove a blue Volvo and was known for careening around curves and challenging the speed limits. She'd pick up at a moment's notice and say, "I'm off to England," and she'd get in her car and drive all day and night up through Switzerland and France and hop the ferry over to England and continue the drive on up to the school there. If she was in a hurry, she took a plane.

I first met her on the day the boarding students arrived for the opening of school. She was holding a tea on her patio, and people were mingling in and out. Uncle Max said that I had to go along with him and Aunt Sandy, that Mrs. Stirling was "very eager" to meet me. I couldn't imagine why, and it made me nervous to think that she might take one look at me and say, "Off with her head!"

But she wasn't anything like that at all. She took both my hands in hers and said I had a charming name and a charming face and she was enormously pleased that I was at her school, and she was enormously pleased that Uncle Max and Aunt Sandy were there, too.

I thought maybe she was a figurehead, like the Queen in England, and that maybe she didn't really do anything, but I was wrong about that. Uncle Max said, "She knows everything that goes on, and if she doesn't like it, she says, 'Change it!' or 'Fix it!' And she means, now, instantly!" He looked a bit intimidated by that.

"But I thought you were the boss," I said.

"No," he said. "She's the boss, and I'm glad of it."

"Why?"

"Because she knows what she's doing. I might not always agree with her—we'll see—but she's got good instincts. Look at what she's pulled together here—" He waved his arm across the campus beyond, taking in the villa, the rolling lawns, the indoor pool and dormitories, the parents and students of mixed nationalities wandering here and there. "She started with nothing and with only two students, her own children. Now look—"

Mrs. Stirling breezed toward us, fishing in the bodice of her dress as she did so. From within her dress, she retrieved a tube of lipstick, which she opened and applied (without a mirror—that impressed me) and then stuffed the lipstick back inside her dress. "Dear," she said to Uncle Max. "See if you can find that charming family who came all the way from Osaka this morning. I think there is a problem about the tuition. Will you fix it up with the business office?"

She smiled down on me. "Domenica—such a lovely name!"

"Do you really have a house in Italy?" I asked her.

"I do! And it's in the most perfect spot in the

world and you must come there with me some day soon. You and Max and Sandy."

"And where is it in Italy?" I asked.

But she wasn't able to answer because she'd spotted Guthrie. "Peter, darling!" she called. *Peter?* Had I gotten his name wrong?

Peter/Guthrie blushed and came toward her.

Mrs. Stirling tapped his name tag, which read *Guthrie.* "Dear, you have a perfectly lovely first name. Why must you insist on being called by your last name?" She patted my shoulder. "Domenica, dear, have you met Peter? Peter Lombardy Guthrie the Third."

"Guthrie," he mumbled at me.

"Peter is the most charming young man," Mrs. Stirling said. "A prince!"

Guthrie did not seem all that thrilled to be called a prince, but he smiled at Mrs. Stirling.

"Guthrie!" a voice called. From behind him stepped Lila. "Oh hi, stranger," she said to me.

Stranger? This hit me wrong. Why was *I* the stranger? I was no more a stranger than she was. It reminded me of all the times in all the towns in all the schools when I'd walk in and someone would say "Who's the stranger?" and they'd all look at me as if I were exactly that, *strange*. At the same time I'd be looking at them and wondering who all these strangers were.

"My name's Dinnie," I reminded Lila.

"I know *that*," she said.

She was wearing a white cotton dress and sandals and looked very clean. I'd slopped most of a cherry tart on my sleeve.

"And who are you, my dear?" Mrs. Stirling said, cupping Lila's chin in her hand.

A stranger, I wanted to say. *She's a complete and total stranger. Just like me.*

Lila reached up and tugged at a tiny pearl earring. "I'm Lila," she said. "I'm American."

"But of course you are," Mrs. Stirling said.

"Are you the owner of this place?" Lila said.

"This *place*?" Mrs. Stirling said. She sounded offended. "This *school*, you mean? I am the founder."

"And the owner, right?" Lila said.

Mrs. Stirling turned to Uncle Max. "Oh, these Americans, how direct they can be," she said.

"Could I talk to you about my room?" Lila pressed.

Mrs. Stirling waved at someone across the patio. "Max?" Mrs. Stirling said. "Perhaps you'll assist this young lady with rooming questions?" She smiled at each of us, and moved on to another group.

By the time Uncle Max straggled home that evening, he had a list of twenty-three things that Mrs. Stirling had requested be fixed or changed.

"She doesn't miss a trick!" Aunt Sandy said.

"We've got our work cut out for us," Uncle Max said, but he didn't seem deflated. Instead he seemed revved up, charged, as if he wanted to get the year under way and he wanted it to be brilliant, as brilliant as Mrs. Stirling expected it to be.

He reminded me of my mother, of how excited and eager she would be each time we reached a new town. "We'd better get busy!" my mother would say. "Lots to do!"

I asked Aunt Sandy if she knew where in Italy Mrs. Stirling's house was.

She was trying to read the directions on a cake mix. "Not exactly. Somewhere near Florence, I think," she said. "I have no idea what these directions say. I either have to add two eggs or two something-elses. Would you hand me the Italian dictionary?"

Because Mrs. Stirling had a house in Italy, I linked her with my grandma Fiorelli. Maybe they'd known each other once. Maybe I'd see where Grandma Fiorelli grew up. And even though I realized that my grandma Fiorelli didn't know me any better than Aunt Sandy or Uncle Max did, I still wanted to go to the place my grandma had lived. If I went there, maybe someone would see me and say, "Oh I know who you are! You are the granddaughter of Mrs. Fiorelli!"

And I would walk the streets where my grandma had walked, and I'd go into the house where she had lived, and I'd be home.

Back in the kitchen with Aunt Sandy, I said, "Do you know where Grandma Fiorelli lived in Italy? You know where she came from?"

Aunt Sandy was picking eggshells out of the bowl. "Ma? Where she came from? Good question. Campo-something. I forget."

"Mrs. Stirling invited us to go to her house in Italy, did you hear her?"

"I heard. But I think I'm going to have to

practice my manners first. And I want to wait and see if we still have jobs come next week. I'm not sure I'm up to all this." She glanced across the room at Uncle Max, who was sitting at the table, working on his list. "But I hope *he* is," she said. "It scares me half to death, the responsibility of several hundred teenagers day and night." She shuddered. "I can't even remember to feed the cat!"

"You don't have a cat," I said.

"See! I can't even remember I don't have a cat!"

8

⌁ An Italian Tongue ⌁

Guthrie was like an electric cloud of whirling energy. He loved everything—classes, sports, field trips, food, people. But most of all, he loved Switzerland. "*Svizzera!*" he would boom. "*Bella, bella, Svizzera!*" He reminded me a little of my father, the way he bounded around, full of enthusiasm.

I asked Guthrie how to say *kidnapped* in Italian and I went home and made a sign, but Aunt Sandy said, "I think what you've written means *haircut.* You might get people knocking at the door for a haircut."

I tried another spelling of what I thought Guthrie had said. Aunt Sandy flipped through my dictionary. "That means *turnip.* Or *blockhead.*"

Guthrie was American. He'd been at the school for two years and knew loads of Italian, but it was Guthrie's own version of Italian, Uncle Max said.

"Guthrie fractures the language sometimes, but nobody seems to mind too much because he does it with such gusto."

I was mesmerized by people who could speak Italian. I'd watch little kids strolling along the lake with their parents, jabbering away in Italian. It seemed so clever of them. I knew this was their only language, the one they'd learned from birth, but still it seemed as if it were an incredible talent. When I heard a boy command his dog to sit: *Siediti!*, and the dog obeyed, I thought, *Wow, even the dog knows Italian.*

Me, I stumbled along tossing out the few words I knew: *ciao!* (which sounded like *chow* and meant both hello and good-bye), and *andiamo!* (let's go). I knew how to start a question, like *Dov'è* . . . (Where is . . . ?), but I didn't know the words that came after, so I'd end up saying things like "*Dov'è* the bus station?" and people would look at me blankly. And even when I did manage to get out a whole question in Italian, their answers sounded like *mumble mumble-ino.*

In school most of us took Italian lessons. Three days a week we studied grammar, and it was painful, painful. I didn't get it at all. My brain would not accept that the spelling of a word such as *red* would change, depending on what it was describing. Sometimes *red* was *rossa*, sometimes *rosso*. And the innocent little word *a* was sometimes *una*, sometimes *uno*, sometimes *un*.

A red car was *una macchina rossa*, but a red boat was *un battello rosso*. Some nouns (like car, *una macchina*) were feminine; some nouns (like boat, *un battello*) were masculine. How did you figure out which words were masculine and which were feminine? Why was a car feminine and a boat masculine? Why wasn't everything neutral? How did those little Italian kids learn all this?

"Just memorize," the teacher said. "Memorize."

I'd picture a car with lipstick and a boat with a moustache, in order to remember which was feminine and which was masculine.

Two days a week we had conversation in Italian. We'd memorize dialogues and act them out. If you thought about what you were saying, you'd feel stupid, but if you just concentrated on the sounds and the rhythm, it was better. You didn't want to think that you were sitting there all morning saying, "I have a red pen and a blue pen. I have two pens. How many pens do you have?" If you thought very hard about what you were really saying you'd feel like a dolt.

According to my teacher, I had told her I went to bed at *seven hundred o'clock,* and that I was *three hundred and thirty years old.* She said I'd just asked my classmate *How much does the time cost?* and *I want six hundred potatoes, no thank you.*

Had my Grandma Fiorelli really spoken this language, and had she really not known any English when she'd come to America, and had it been hard for her to learn English? I wondered about these things from time to time.

And then I'd wonder about all the foreign students in this American school—all the Japanese and Spanish and French and Norwegian and Indian and Saudi Arabian and Iranian and German and Dutch and Chinese—how could they study whole subjects like history and algebra and science in English, a completely different language from their own?

When they asked me "How to discover them gym?" or "Do you habit America?" they were making more sense in English than I was in Italian.

At night when I tried to study my Italian, sometimes I'd get so mad at not being able to remember how to say something that I'd throw my book across my bedroom. Aunt Sandy would hear the thud and tap at my door. "Studying Italian again?" she'd say. She was sympathetic because she'd come home with a botched haircut. She hadn't been able to explain what she'd wanted.

I got only one compliment from my Italian teacher, although I didn't know it was a compliment at the time. She told me I had "an Italian tongue." It seemed like an insult, but Guthrie said it meant that my pronunciation was good. I wondered if that was because I'd heard my mother say some of these words, if maybe the sound was fixed in my brain.

. . . .

The Dreams of Domenica Santolina Doone

I got a sackful of letters from my parents and from Stella and Crick. The letters were in Italian and I couldn't read them. *I showed the letters to everyone, but no one else could read them either. "It's not real Italian," they said. There were pictures in with some of the letters, but I couldn't see them. They were very, very black. "They must be in Italian," I thought.*

. . . .

9

⌇: Toes and Teeth :~

I got two more postcards from Aunt Grace and Aunt Tillie.

Dear Dinnie,

    Thanks for your card. I never got a stamp from Switzerland before! I don't understand why you have to speak Italian, you're not in Italy. I hope you go fishing soon.

    Lonnie's toe operation didn't turn out so good, but he went to a specialist so they don't have to amputate, which is a great relief to him, I can assure you.

    I'm on my way to Tillie's. I'm taking her some pot roast because she don't know how to make it right.

    Here come a gazillion hugs—

    Love, love, love,

    Your Aunt Grace

And Tillie's card said:

Dear Dinnie,

Your daddy will get over it, don't you worry. It is just hard to raise a child and see them fly the coop but it's a good thing.

I had a picture of Stella's baby, it's real cute.

Maybe you should just go fishing by yourself.

I'm getting my teeth fixed and I'm gonna look just like Marilyn Monroe!

Gotta go make some jello. Grace is coming over, bringing some of that awful pot roast with her. Don't tell her I told you that.

Multiply these two kisses times a billion and that's how many I send you: xx

Love from your Aunt Tillie, Champion Cheesecake Jello Maker

10

～ Complaints ～

Lila no longer thought that everything was "amazing" and "incredible." Now it was all "horrid." Sometimes I wondered if she was purposely trying to make people dislike her. She'd begun on the second day of school, when she had demanded a change in roommates. Lila had been assigned a room with Belen, a returning student.

"I can't understand a word she says," Lila complained.

"You will, soon enough," the dorm resident said.

Lila phoned her parents in Saudi to complain. She pounded on Uncle Max's office door. "My parents aren't paying all this money for me to be in a room with someone who doesn't even speak English!" she said. "If I'd known I'd have to actually live with a Spanish foreigner, I wouldn't have come here, that's for sure. I want an American roommate."

I heard about most of this at home. Uncle Max had told me that I'd probably hear things that I'd have to keep confidential. I'd have to act as if I didn't know anything I'd heard at home. "There are things," Uncle Max had said, "that I'll probably need to unload to Sandy, and you may hear them. If it bothers you, let me know."

When I overheard about Lila and her roommate, I said, "Why can't she have an American roommate?"

Uncle Max said that the whole purpose of the school was to mix the students. "Lila will end up learning some Spanish, and learning some things about Belen. And Belen will learn some English and some things about Lila. Lila will settle down. You'll see."

But Lila didn't settle down. For a week, she appeared at Uncle Max's office each day, demanding a room change.

"Where do you get all that patience?" Aunt Sandy asked him. "Honestly, I could never do what you do. I'd be leaping up and down and telling those kids to quit moaning. I'd be fired in one day if I had your job."

At the end of the week, I asked Uncle Max again, "Why don't you just change her room?"

"Belen's a nice girl. She and Lila will end up best friends. You'll see."

The following Monday, Lila stormed out of Uncle Max's office and skipped the rest of her classes. She phoned her parents, she phoned Uncle Max at home that night, she threw Belen's clothes on the floor, and she hounded her dorm resident.

Now Belen was mad, and she, too, demanded a room change. And then suddenly, after three more days of storming and fuming, Lila switched gears. She'd found other things to worry about. The food, according to Lila, was "disgusting." She passed around a petition, which few people signed, demanding "real American hamburger and real American cereal." In the dining hall, she'd say to the kitchen staff, "How can you *serve* this slop?" To other students, she'd say, "How can you *eat* this slop?"

When Lila found out that she, like all the rest of us, had to do four hours of community service each week—chores like waiting tables, moving books, tutoring, or visiting a hospital, she refused. To the teacher in charge of community service, Lila said, "This is slave labor. My parents aren't paying all this money for me to work for *you*."

When she received a detention for skipping her community service, she skipped the detention and phoned her parents, who, in turn, phoned Uncle Max. He explained the school's philosophy behind helping in the community and assigned Lila two more detentions.

It was the same with Lila and the sports requirement. She had signed up for tennis, but was assigned swimming because tennis was full. "Get another tennis coach," she told the sports director. "My parents aren't paying all this money for me to take a sport I don't *like*."

"You'll just *love* swimming," the sports director said.

Other students called her a spoiled brat behind her back, and they stayed clear of her. When her name was mentioned at our house, Uncle Max rubbed his forehead, and Aunt Sandy would say, "What's that girl up to now?"

Sometimes I made excuses for Lila. I listened

to her complaints. She didn't seem at all bothered that she was insulting my uncle when she insulted the school. She'd say, "Honestly, *they* don't know what they're doing," and "*They* don't care about anything," and "*They* won't listen to me." *They* sometimes referred to all the teachers, but it always included my uncle, the headmaster. Often she'd say, "Why doesn't he do something about that?"

People asked me how I could stand her and why I was her friend. I didn't know the answers to those questions. Part of me was still holding on to that first image I'd had of Lila—of the laughing, friendly girl. And now, when I was with her, I felt as if that was where I was supposed to be. It never occurred to me to walk away from her or tell her to shut up. Being with Lila was like watching a movie. You couldn't believe she was actually doing and saying some of these things, but you stuck around to see what would happen next.

At home sometimes I felt as if I were two people. When Uncle Max described Lila's behavior, I was embarrassed for Lila and sorry for Uncle Max's headaches over her. But when I listened to Lila, I'd find myself nodding along with her, feeling the unfairness of it all.

Once when I tried to give Uncle Max's side of things, Lila said, "Honestly, Dinnie, I don't know why you defend him. Honestly, sometimes I think you don't like me at all!"

Like her? I hadn't really thought about whether I liked her or not. She was just Lila.

"You're so lucky," she said.

"Lucky? Me?"

"You've got your family," she said, and she burst into tears.

I couldn't explain that my real family was thousands of miles away on a hilltop in New Mexico—or were they? Had they moved on by now? Would they tell me when they moved?

I couldn't tell her that my real family had shipped me off like a spare parcel, and as far as I knew, they hardly realized I was gone. I couldn't tell her that I thought about them day and night, night and day, and that I felt as if I was drifting, floating, lost in the air. And I couldn't understand why Lila had spent the past month attacking Uncle Max and now was telling me I was lucky to have him.

"*You* don't have to be alone," she sobbed.

"Oh," I said. "You feel like you're alone?"

She hit me. "Isn't that what I just said?"

"Not exactly—"

"I don't believe it! Now you're going to argue with me? Now? When I'm feeling so terrible and alone—"

I invited her to dinner. Maybe she just missed being in a home. It would be nice for her, and I was glad I'd thought of such a good idea.

It was not a good idea. When I told Aunt Sandy that I'd invited Lila for dinner that same evening, Aunt Sandy said, "But Dinnie—I've got essays to grade and reports to do—and Max has so much work. And I was just going to throw something together—"

"Lila won't mind," I said.

"Are you kidding?" Aunt Sandy said. "This is the girl who got a petition up against the school's *slop!*"

11

⌐: It's So Rude :~

When Uncle Max straggled home at six o'clock, he had five minutes' warning about Lila coming to dinner. On hearing the news, he winced, glanced at his briefcase, and said, "Guess I'd better go wash up then."

Lila chattered from the minute she stepped through the door. I thought this was a good sign, that she was making an effort to be friendly. Even Uncle Max and Aunt Sandy seemed relieved that she wasn't complaining.

But it all fell apart at the dinner table.

"The Japanese drive me crazy," Lila said, swooping up every single Japanese student in one lump and dumping them on the table.

"All of them?" Aunt Sandy asked.

"All of them," Lila insisted. "They never look at you. It's so rude."

"But in their country," Aunt Sandy said, "maybe it's rude to—"

"They're not in *their* country, are they?" Lila said. "I mean if they don't want to look at people while they're in their own country, well, who's to stop them? But they're *here*. They're with Americans."

"More potatoes?" I asked.

"I can't tell any of them apart," Lila said.

At first I thought she meant the potatoes, but the look on Uncle Max's face made it clear that she was still talking about the Japanese.

"They probably have the same trouble with the Americans," Uncle Max said.

"I don't see how," Lila said. "We all look *different*."

Aunt Sandy asked what language Lila was studying. You could choose another language, in addition to the required Italian, if you wanted.

"That Italian stuff I have to take," Lila said, "and Spanish, but I'm changing at semester. I hate Spanish. I used to like it, but now that I'm around all these Spanish kids, I hate it. Do you know what they do? They talk in Spanish all the time. It's so rude."

The Italians, she said, "dress too flashy. It's

like they're trying to show us how much money they have. And they're so loud. It's so rude."

The Germans were too pushy and apparently too smart. "Do you know what they do in my history class?" Lila said. "They answer everything. They don't give anyone a chance to think. It's so rude."

On and on she went, trashing the Swedes, the French, the Iranians. She managed to cover most of the nationalities in the school. At last, Uncle Max said, "Well, at least there are the Americans. I suppose you're glad there are Americans here, too?"

Lila chewed for a moment. "I don't mean to be critical, what with you being the headmaster and all, but I thought this was an American school—"

"It is," Uncle Max said.

"No, it isn't. It's full of people who aren't American."

"The majority are American," Uncle Max said. "The school is American in courses, in philosophy, in—"

"Whatever," Lila said. "Besides, the Americans

who are here aren't really American."

"Aren't really American?" Aunt Sandy said. I could tell that Aunt Sandy was annoyed. She looked as if she were holding herself in her chair in order to keep from leaping over the table and strangling Lila.

In my mind, I had already tied Lila's scarf around her mouth in order to silence her.

"Aren't really American?" Aunt Sandy repeated.

"No," Lila instructed. "Most of them haven't even lived in the States for years and years. Most of them have lived all over the world. Hardly any of them care if a person is American or not."

"You think people should care that you're American, is that it?" Uncle Max asked. "They should notice—?"

"Yes," Lila said. "Yes, they should. Because if this is an American school, then the Americans should be, well, you know—" She stared down at her plate. "Everybody just shouldn't be so rude, especially not to Americans."

I'd been waiting for a chance to jump into the conversation, and finally I leaped in with, "Lila probably feels like a stranger here. It's awful to feel like the stranger."

I turned to Lila, expecting her to toss me a smile of gratitude, or a look of grateful astonishment at the depth of my understanding and sympathy. She didn't smile. Instead she said, icily, "I do *not* feel like a stranger, Dinnie! That's completely ridiculous."

In my mind, I dumped the potatoes in her lap.

I walked her back to her dorm. At the door, she said, "Do you think your aunt and uncle liked me?"

"Sure," I lied. "Sure they did."

12

~: Nomads and Cuckoos :~

The Dreams of Domenica Santolina Doone

I was in my bubble and it was getting bigger and bigger, stretching from all the stuff that was coming in the pores. Italian words were floating around inside the bubble, bumping into Japanese words and Spanish words. The bubble wall was getting thinner and thinner. I was afraid it would pop, but it didn't. I woke up.

Most students stayed about as far away from Lila as they could get, but Guthrie didn't mind her one bit. "She's a pistol," Guthrie would say, "a real pistol," and he'd laugh when he said it.

If Lila were coming down the walk, someone would inevitably mutter, "Here comes the witch," but Guthrie would say, loud enough for Lila to hear, "Watch out everybody. Here comes the pistol. Better duck." He'd smile and stand right in her path. "Is it loaded?" he'd say. "Spare me, Lila, spare me—"

"Very funny, Guthrie," Lila would say. "Very amusing, I'm sure." But she liked it, I could tell. She'd toss her hair back and smile at Guthrie.

Lila and Guthrie were in two classes together. I didn't have any classes with her, and only one with Guthrie. Often I saw them walking together after class, and what surprised me was that Guthrie was usually doing the talking while Lila listened. When I was with Lila, she talked—or complained—and I listened.

And sometimes when I was listening, I'd think of things my sister Stella had said. Stella had kept a journal of all the places we'd lived and had recorded things she'd learned in each town. There was one whole page from when we lived in Ohio, about how to take a bus. In Indiana, she wrote: *Don't talk. Just listen.*

"What does that mean?" I asked her. "Why not talk?"

"Because people will laugh at your accent. Just listen. Wait and see how people talk and then talk like them."

In Oklahoma, Stella wrote, *Expect the worst.*

"Why?" I asked. "Why expect the worst?"

"Because then," Stella said, "you'll be prepared. You won't be caught off guard."

I figured that because Stella was older, she knew what she was talking about, and I followed her advice. I listened, and I expected the worst, most of the time.

In Oregon she wrote, *Dress plain the first day.*

"Why?" I asked.

"Because if you wear cowboy boots in Oregon, people are going to laugh at you. Wait and see what people wear, and then dress like them."

My mother overheard this. She said, "Stella! What a boring way to live. Don't you want to be different from everybody else?"

"No, I do not," Stella said. "I want to be the same."

Sometimes I wanted to be the same, because then you'd have friends, and you wouldn't be just the new kid, but inside, deep inside my bubble, I also wanted to be different. I wanted to be interesting, but I didn't know how you got to be interesting.

Guthrie was different and he was interesting, and so was Lila. What I liked about them was that Guthrie was complete Guthrie through and through, and Lila was Lila through and through.

Guthrie was like no one else. He'd be walking down the hill and all of a sudden, he'd shout *"Sono libero!"* (I am free!) He pronounced *libero* like this: *LEE-bear-oh.* *"Libero, libero, liberooooooo!"*

He'd dive into the pool and shout, *"Fantastico!"* People liked being around him because when you were around him, you were happy, and you felt as if you could do anything he could do.

Lila was different in other ways, in ways that made people hate her much of the time. But what I thought was interesting about her was that she was always Lila. She knew what she thought and she wasn't afraid to say what she thought, even if it was wrong or stupid or mean, although she her-self never thought that what she said was wrong or stupid or mean. She thought that she was right and that everyone else was wrong, and she didn't seem to care if she had friends or not.

I'd always felt as if I were in a sort of suspen-sion, waiting to see how things worked, waiting to see who I was and what sort of life I might lead, and then moving on to a new town before I could figure out any of those things. Lila and Guthrie, though, seemed to already know who they were and they were already living their lives.

Sometimes Lila would say, "I'm the kind of person who—" and she'd finish that sentence in various ways: "I'm the kind of person who needs a room of my own"; and "I'm the kind of person who needs to talk about my feelings"; and "I'm the kind of person who has to have time to think." And every time she'd say something like this, I'd wonder how she came to know what kind of person she was.

I felt like Miss Average. I was neither tall nor short, neither chubby nor slim. People often said I had nice eyes, but no one knew what color they were. "Are those hazel? Brownish? Gray? What color is that, anyway?" Teachers often said I had "a sweet face," but when I looked in the mirror, it didn't look all that sweet to me. On my report cards, teachers usually wrote things like *Coming along* and *Satisfactory work* and *Very observant* and *Ought to speak up more.*

I was all jumbled up most places, but especially here in Switzerland because it didn't seem to be like any place I'd ever lived. This wasn't just another new town and this wasn't just another new school. Here everybody was from different places, not just me. Most of the people were new, not just me. Everybody had a different accent, not just me. At the beginning, you looked at people, and you'd think, "He's Japanese," or "She's Spanish," but after a couple weeks, you forgot about that and you'd think, "There's Keisuke," or "That's Belen," and if someone were to say to you at the beginning of school, "Where's that person from?" you'd probably make a pretty good guess: Japan, Spain, China, India, but after a couple months if someone asked you that, you wouldn't be able to answer.

You'd first have to stop and think, "Let's see, Keisuke, his parents live in Osaka, but he was born in Lagos—" And people who looked Japanese might be American and never have lived in Japan, and people who looked Spanish might have been born in India of Spanish parents, and might have lived in Spain later for a couple years, but then gone on to live in Nigeria or Sweden or Belgium.

If someone asked me where I was from, I could just say, "the States." I didn't have to go into that whole long story of my first life, about how I was born in Kentucky but then lived in Virginia and North Carolina and Tennessee and on and on and on. I wasn't the only nomad here. Lots of people were nomads. Nomads were normal!

During the class day there was a dress code, and everyone dressed pretty much the same, not in uniforms, but in plain clothes. The boys wore sport coats and ties and plain slacks; the girls wore skirts or slacks, and regular tops. Jeans weren't allowed during the school day. After school you could dress however you liked and it didn't matter if you didn't dress like anyone else. Everyone borrowed everyone else's clothes, and so you'd see people wearing an odd mishmash: a roommate's Saudi scarf with someone else's T-shirt printed with a Spanish slogan and American jeans and Italian shoes.

I liked this, because during the school day when everyone dressed pretty much alike, you didn't have to worry that your shoes or your clothes were uncool, and after school, no matter what you wore, someone else thought it was terrific because it was different from what they had. In my other schools, the first month after I'd arrive was always the worst, as I frantically tried to figure out if socks were in or out, and if people were going to make fun of my shoes or my clothes.

The classes at the Swiss school were small, no more than fifteen students, and some of my classes only had ten students in them. The teachers knew everyone's name by the second day, and you couldn't hide in the back or in the crowd. If you hadn't done your homework, it was real obvious, and so you did your homework, and you spent more time on it because you didn't want to be discovered to be completely lacking in brains.

At my other schools, my teachers would eventually discover that I had huge gaps in my knowledge. Somewhere along the way, I'd missed learning how to multiply and divide; I'd learned about nouns and pronouns but only had a vague idea what an adverb was; and although I could have described dozens of towns all across America, I'd never learned the state capital cities.

But at the school in Switzerland, with new students zooming in each year, coming from all over the world, from all sorts of schools, it seemed that there wasn't a lot of common knowledge that could be taken for granted. Some students my age knew calculus, but others, like me, were still struggling with multiplication and division. Some were fluent in three or four languages, but some, like me, were still trying to figure out what an adverb was in their own—and only—language. At least I could speak and write English, so in most of my classes, I felt as if I had a head start over those whose native language wasn't English.

If you were having trouble in something, you could go see a teacher during a free period, and the teacher would explain things to you. Sometimes they'd even introduce you to an upper school student who was really good in whatever subject you were having trouble in, and the older student would help you.

When I was having trouble in geometry (starting about the second day of class), my geometry teacher introduced me to Sonal, a sophomore girl.

Every day during my afternoon study hall, Sonal would sit down with me and show me miracles. I couldn't understand her accent at first, but it didn't seem to matter because she drew things and cut things out and shuffled them around and it made sense that way.

Another thing that was different about this school was that it was cool to study and to try out for the play or the soccer team or swim team. It was cool to take art or photography even if you weren't "artistic," and it was cool to sign up for weekend trips and go hiking or skiing. You could go to Florence on an art history trip and stand around and learn about paintings and architecture. You could go to Milan and see an opera.

We read a poem by Herman Hesse and then the whole class trooped up to Montagnola to see the house in which he'd written that poem, and then the whole class trooped down the hill to the St. Abbondio cemetery and stood at his grave.

These weren't nerdy things to do. In some of my other schools, it had been cool to go to the mall or to the movies or parties. It was cool to take a test without studying. It was cool to drink and smoke and swear. Those things were definitely not cool at this school in Switzerland.

If you got caught drinking or smoking here, you got suspended, and for most students this was dire punishment, because it meant their parents had to pay for them to fly home (even to Japan) to wait out their suspension, and then fly back, and I don't know anybody's parents who were very thrilled about that. If you got caught with even a piece of drug paraphernalia on you, you got expelled. Just like that.

At first I thought this was severe and cruel. In the first month of school, four students were suspended and one expelled. But after that, nothing. It was easier for students to refuse temptation. They could say, "No thanks, my parents would *kill* me if I got suspended/expelled."

Uncle Max made a speech about how drugs and alcohol did not mix with education. He said we were here to learn. If we wanted to mess around with our bodies and our brains, we could do that somewhere else. It might have sounded a bit corny if someone else had said it, but Uncle Max had a way of saying it that made you think he wanted you to be a healthy, decent human being, as if he really cared what happened to you.

I'm not trying to suggest that everything was perfect about this school, because it wasn't. Not every student was friendly, and not every teacher was kind. During the second week of school, one scowling boy who was standing behind me in the dining hall line, said, "Don't take that last taco. If you do, I'll chop your hand off." In the gym one day, a girl asked me if I had a comb, and when I handed mine to her, she immediately stuffed it in her purse and walked away.

My science teacher was Mr. Koo (at home, Aunt Sandy called him Mr. Cuckoo), and on the first day of class he talked for forty-five minutes solid: "I don't want to hear any whining or moaning or complaining from you wimps, and don't you even think about crying or running to the headmaster or your parents to tell them I'm too mean. I've been here for a long time, and I've seen headmasters come and I've seen headmasters go, and believe me, if it comes to a fight between me and the headmaster, I'll win. And I don't want to see anyone messing with the Bunsen burners or

I'll string you up by your toes, and if you break anything, you'll pay for it, and . . ."

On and on and on he went.

So not everyone was kind and not everyone was friendly, but most people were, and even more startling than that was that so many people wanted to show you how to do things—not things like how to burn down a barn or smoke a joint or steal a bike—but things like how to swim or develop film or climb a mountain.

My mouth was hanging half open most of the time.

13

∴ Val Verzasca ∾

One weekend I was on a school trip to Val Verzasca with Guthrie, Belen, and Keisuke. The chaperone was our Italian teacher, Signora Palermo. She was young and wore jeans and a T-shirt which said *Viva Italia!* I liked the way she said *Viva: VEE-vuh!* She punched the air twice with her fist when she said it: *VEE-vuh!* (punch, punch) *VEE-vuh!* (punch, punch).

It was October, but we were having a sudden hot spell. We climbed an arched Roman bridge and leaped off it, down into the clear cool green water. Guthrie shouted *"Viva Verzasca! Sono libero, libero, liberooooo—"*

Keisuke said he didn't want to jump. "That's stupid," he said, but he pronounced it *stew-pod.* Then he jumped and laughed all the way down, but when he bobbed up, he pretended he hadn't liked it. "That was *stew-pod.*"

We climbed over plains of granite—gray

swirls of stone, smooth and cool, with puddles of water trapped in bowls of rock. We hiked across a grassy ridge and all around us were the tall jagged mountains, beige and purple in the haze. And all the way back in the school van, we spoke Italian, and if anyone made a mistake, Signora Palermo would say, "Are you being a *stew-pod?*"

It took us forever to get home because Guthrie kept thinking of places we had to see. *"Signora!"* he'd say, *"Ferma la macchina, per favore!"* (Stop the car, please!) And he'd point out a vineyard terraced all the way up a hill, row upon row of grapevines as far as you could see. *"Fantastico!"* he'd say. *"Puramente fantastico!"*

Guthrie asked Signora Palermo to turn down a narrow lane and then stop at a rocky hill overlooking a clear river. He made us all climb out of the van and breathe the air. "I am a transparent eyeball!" he shouted. It sounded very funny at the time. "It's from Emerson," Guthrie said. "He was into nature in a big way, and he'd go out in the woods and he felt transparent, like he was nothing and yet he could see everything and was a part of everything: one big huge transparent eyeball! Wow!"

Guthrie made Signora Palermo stop at a castle in Bellinzona and made us rub our hands across the old, old stone. He made her stop in Locarno for *gelato*, the smooth, creamy ice cream that slid down your throat. We'd be riding along and he'd shout, "*Guardate!* Look—look—" and he'd point out a thin waterfall streaming down the side of a cliff or a man leading his cows across the hills or a bell tower or a village perched on a mountain.

And all the way, I was having double vision. I'd look at what Guthrie was pointing at and I'd see something else laid thinly over it, like a transparent photo. The grapevines on a Swiss hillside were overlaid with grapevines I'd seen in Ohio, along a winding road, near a lake. The castle slid behind an image of a stone tower I'd seen in Virginia. Even the *gelato* was submerged beneath an ice cream cone I'd eaten in Wisconsin, walking down State Street with Stella and Crick.

It was as if I were carrying around all the places I'd ever lived, and nothing I was seeing was just what it was—it was all of the places, all smooshed together. My bubble was fairly bursting by the time I got home, what with all that stuff crammed in there.

14

~: Goober :~

In the middle of October, I finally got a letter from my mother in which she said, among other things, that she wasn't much of a letter writer, but that she beamed me good thoughts every day. Inside the envelope was a wee picture she'd painted. It was of a girl fishing by a river, and the girl was me.

My father, she said, was "exploring a new opportunity," but she didn't say what it was. Stella was learning that "being a mother is hard work," but the baby was "real real real cute."

I carried the letter in my pocket for weeks, until it ended up in the washing machine with my jeans. And even then, although it was bleached of most of its writing, I ironed it and placed it in my top desk drawer, where I'd see it each day.

The same day I got my mother's letter, I got a postcard from Crick, and one each from Aunt Grace and Aunt Tillie. This was Crick's:

Hi, Dinnie, you little goober—
I miss you. Hope you are being better than me.
How much does it cost to mail a postcard to
Switzerland? I guess I'll find out.
Love from Crick, your Cool Dude brother

And Aunt Grace's:

Dear Dinnie,
It sounds like maybe you're not still feeling like a
prisoner? Been fishing yet?
Lonnie's toe is okay, thanks for asking, just a little
purple. I got a bum knee.
Tillie's coming over tonight. I'm gonna try some of
my apricot chicken on her. It's real good.
This is soaked in a bazillion hugs—
Love, love, love,
Your Aunt Grace

And Tillie's card said:

Dear Dinnie,
Your daddy frets, but that's your daddy. He don't
show anybody, but I know when he's fretting.

Did you find a river yet?

My teeth didn't end up like Marilyn Monroe's but they look pretty good. Take care of your teeth, honey.

Gotta get on my scooter (ha ha, I don't really have a scooter) and get on over to Grace's. She says she's cooking up something with apricots. Lord have mercy!

Seven billion kisses,

Love from your Aunt Tillie, Champion Cheesecake Jello Maker

15

⌐: *Percorso* :~

One Saturday, Guthrie appeared at our door and said, "Get your tennis shoes on! We're going on an expedition!"

I followed him up the path through Montagnola and down the narrow lane beyond, and three miles along, we came to a sign that said PERCORSO. A path led into the woods.

Guthrie started running, "Come on," he said, "the rule is you have to run this. Don't worry, there are places you have to stop, too."

So I ran along behind him, and in the woods the trees were golden and the path was golden from the leaves which had already fallen. About a quarter-mile along the path, Guthrie stopped. There was a sign beside a climbing frame made of thick branches.

"See?" he said. "It tells you here what to do. Beginners cross it three times, intermediates cross it six times, and advanced cross it ten times.

Watch." He scrambled up the frame and reached for the ladder which was balanced across the top. Hand-over-hand he made his way across and jumped down at the end. "Your turn!"

I did three crossings; Guthrie did ten. And then we continued on. At regular intervals along the path were exercise stations. At one you clambered over tree stumps, each one a bit higher than the next, and at another, you walked across a slim beam suspended two feet off the ground, and at another you crossed a swinging bridge.

It was the most amazing thing. It was like a grown-up playground in the woods. Occasionally we met other people doing the *percorso*. We'd hear laughing and squeals and we'd come around a bend, and there would be a married couple or a whole family swinging from branches or tiptoeing across a beam.

We wound all through the woods like this, up and down hills, along cliffs and then veering back into the trees. At one point we came around a bend, and there, lapping at our feet, was the clearest river I'd ever seen. The water rolled and bubbled along over fat stones, and you could see the whole bottom as clear as anything.

"Do you think a person could fish here?" I asked.

"Don't see why not!" Guthrie said.

And on we went, the path looping all through the woods in one big circle so that we ended up back where we began.

"Aren't the Swiss brilliant?" Guthrie said. "To provide such a thing as this, and it's free!"

One of the items in my box of things that I'd carried with me from move to move was a fold-up fishing rod that my father had given me for my eighth birthday. The day after Guthrie had taken me to the *percorso*, I went back on my own, toting my fishing rod.

I cannot even begin to say why I liked fishing so much. I didn't really enjoy the part about catching anything and having to unsnag the hook and apologize to the fish and release it back into the water. Sometimes I didn't even use bait. What I liked was casting the line and then sitting there, watching the water.

First I'd see the water and the banks, and then

if it was clear like this river, I'd examine the bottom, and then I'd look at the riverbank and the trees, and then it would happen. I would see things that weren't outside of me, but were inside me. And that day as I sat on the riverbank, what I saw was my father and my mother and Stella and Crick and the new baby and even Aunt Tillie and Aunt Grace. One by one, I saw them. They were in my mind, but they were more real here, as if they were floating out in front of me, rising up from the water.

And while I was seeing them I had two contrasting feelings. One was complete happiness, as if I was back in a comfortable place with people I knew and who knew me. The other feeling was complete and overwhelming homesickness. It was as if the two feelings were taking turns, and I was waiting to see which one would win.

In the end, neither won. They were both still there, but I packed them away inside my bubble and headed home.

16

∿: Bloomable :∿

Keisuke (pronounced *KAY-sue-kee*, he explained, after I'd called him *Kee-sook* for two weeks) was in most of my classes. He was full of surprises. He was slim and quiet, unlike the bounding, talkative, athletic Guthrie, but he and Guthrie were friends and they seemed to balance each other.

Keisuke often acted as if he didn't want to do some of the impulsive things Guthrie suggested, like dashing off on a hiking trip or leaping into a creek or trying new foods, but he'd always go along or try the new foods, and even though he'd say something was *stew-pod* or *dis-goast-ing*, his grin would suggest otherwise.

In class, when he was asked a question, he would scrunch up his mouth and say, "Now that's good question. I think about it." At first I thought this was his way of saying he didn't have a clue as to what the answer was or that he didn't want to talk, but then, about ten minutes later, he'd pop up with something unusual and interesting.

In art history class, when he was asked a question about Picasso, he said, "Now that's good question. I think about it." Ten minutes later, he raised his hand, and, pointing to a painting in our book, said, "It's like geometry," and he went on to explain about shapes and perspective. When he was finished, he said to the teacher, "What you think?" and the teacher said, "I couldn't have said it better myself."

He mangled English, but the words he substituted were often better than the right ones. *Plumpy* seemed a better description than *plump*, and *bloomable* sounded much more interesting than *possible*. When he said *running in my ears the bells*, we knew exactly what he meant, and it seemed exactly the right way of saying how the St. Abbondio bells echoed in your head after they'd stopped ringing.

He and Belen were always together. Belen was outspoken, moody and, as Keisuke put it, "dead-drop beautiful." She was dark-skinned with a long mane of black hair, and at the first dance, when she wore a simple black dress and red lipstick, the boys gaped. She looked eighteen instead of thirteen. Keisuke said, "She knocks my eyeballs."

Belen usually said what was on her mind, or as Keisuke put it, "Holding with salami she doesn't." If she thought she'd received an unfair grade, she'd march up to the teacher and say, "Please explain why this gets only a C." But she wasn't argumentative like Lila was. When she got the explanation, she'd say, "Okay. Next one better, you'll see."

Belen told me that her parents had forbidden her to spend time with Keisuke. When I asked her why, she shrugged. "Because I like him too much." I must have looked puzzled because she added, "I'm too young to like him so much, but I still am going to like him. My parents can't see me here, no?"

Here was someone who was glad her parents couldn't see her, who seemed happy to be making her own way, while I had been wishing that my parents *could* see me. At night I would beam them images of me, thinking, *Here is where I am. Here is what I am doing and what I am thinking. Can you see me?*

For the first time, I thought maybe I should

just get on with it, maybe they didn't have to see me, to actually be there with me. And then I thought how surprising it was that once, not very long ago, Guthrie and Lila and Belen and Keisuke had all been strangers to me, and I to them, but already I felt comfortable with them, and they were becoming as real to me as my family. Was I adapting? Was that a good thing?

I hoped that I wasn't going to forget my family entirely, that I wasn't going to replace them with these other people. Because if I could replace them, then they could replace me, too.

That night I wrote my family a long, long letter, in which I tried to describe the place where I was living and the people I'd met. And then I made a long, long list of all the things I was remembering about them. Finally, because I was feeling very soppy by that time, I added a P. S.: *Don't forget me!*

Before I went to bed, I put a sign in my window: *DOV'È DINNIE?* (Where is Dinnie?)

Uncle Max came in to say goodnight, examined the sign, tilted his head, read it again, looked at me, looked back at the sign, and said, "In a casa on the Via Poporino between Lugano and Montagnola in the Ticino in Switzerland in Europe on the planet Earth." And then he kissed my forehead and smoothed the duvet at my feet and turned out the light.

17

~: Struggles :~

One day in November, I was sitting in English class, doodling in the margins of my notebook. I'd drawn a mountain, with a house perched on its peak. I was just about to add some people to the scene, when I heard Mr. Bonner say that a character in the story we had just read was struggling, and it was that struggling that made the character interesting. He wondered if we agreed with him and if we knew what the character was struggling with.

"Dinnie?" he said. "Any guesses?"

It had been a story about a boy who wants to run faster than anyone else, and so he runs and he runs and he runs, and he enters a race, and he runs like the wind, he runs and runs, faster than he has ever run before. But he doesn't win the race.

"Dinnie?" Mr. Bonner said. "You awake? Any idea what this character is struggling with?"

"He wants something and he can't have it," I said.

"So is he struggling with the thing he wants?"

Keisuke said, "He struggles with legs. Too slow legs!"

Guthrie chimed in. "Himself? Is he struggling with himself? He wants to go faster, but he can't, is that it?"

On and on people went. I found myself listening carefully. It felt as if there was something—right around the corner—maybe in what someone would say next—that was a key to something that mattered to me. Whatever that something was kept slipping away, though.

At the end of class, Mr. Bonner gave us our homework: to write about what our own struggles were. He said that we didn't have to turn this homework in if it was too private, but we had to show him we'd done it.

So that night I spent three hours writing about my struggles. When I started, I couldn't think of any struggles. No struggles! So *that* was why I wasn't interesting.

And then I started thinking of struggling with

moving and figuring out where I was and why my family had sent me away. I wrote about struggling with homesickness and with figuring out who I was. On and on I went. I was full of struggles! And that made me so happy: If I was full of struggles, maybe I was interesting!

. . . .

The Dreams of Domenica Santolina Doone

I was bound up with ropes and chained to a wall, and I kicked and struggled, trying to get loose. I was not going to be defeated! I was going to get free!

A class of students were led past my cell. They pointed at me and said, "Isn't she interesting?"

It made me struggle harder. I was a champion struggling person.

When I woke up, the bedclothes were all in a heap and my pillow was lying on the floor on the other side of the room.

. . . .

18

◡: An Announcement :◡

School was due to break for the holidays mid-December. As the vacation neared, boarders were looking forward to home-cooked meals and reunions with their families, and they were looking beyond that, too, to the promise of the St. Moritz ski term at the end of the holidays, when school resumed.

In January, they would all return to campus and board the buses for St. Moritz for a two-week stay, where academic classes took second-place to ski lessons. Guthrie and other returning students spread the word that this was the highlight of the year. *"Fantastico!"* Guthrie said. *"Meraviglioso! Dynamite!"*

I wasn't looking forward to any of it. I wasn't going home for Christmas because it was too expensive. I'd had only six letters from my mother, none from Stella or Crick or my father. Tucked in one letter were pictures of Stella and the new baby. Was that Stella? Her hair was shorter, her face thinner. I'd find myself talking to the picture: *Is that you, Stella?* and I'd touch the baby's face. *What do you feel like, baby?* The baby had a name, Michael, but it seemed odd to call a wee baby by a grown person's name, and so I called him *baby*, just *baby*.

One night, early in December, as Lila and I were walking back from the library, she said, "I think you should know that I'm not coming back."

The wind raced straight at us, pushing into my face, as if it would push me back over the hillside and down, down, down. "Not coming back?" I said.

"After Christmas. I'm not coming back." Lila pulled her scarf up against her face, and the wind caught the ends and slapped them against my neck.

"But—but—" I pulled her coat sleeve. "Stop—"

"I just thought you should know," Lila said.

Bare branches clicked overhead. "You can't mean that. You'll come back."

"I hate it here," she said.

"You don't—" A notebook lay on the path,

and the wind whipped through its pages.

"I do. Don't tell me what I feel," Lila said. "It's a horrid place. I'm the kind of person who is very sensitive about where I live."

At home, I found Uncle Max in his study, bent over a memo. "Lila isn't coming back," I said. "She hates it here."

"She withdrew from school?" Uncle Max asked.

"Not yet—but she's going to. What are you going to do?"

"I haven't heard anything from her parents about this."

"Maybe they don't know yet," I said. "But she'll convince them. You ought to do—"

"Dinnie, do you know how many students say this at the end of the first term? It happens all the time."

"But she hates it here—"

"And when she goes home," Uncle Max said, "to the place and the people she has romanticized all these months, she'll see that it isn't all she imagined. She'll be different, but they'll all expect her to be the same. She'll start thinking about school, and she'll see some of the good things about being here. She'll—"

Aunt Sandy appeared in the doorway. "I'd like to give that girl a good shake, that's what I'd like to do."

It seemed a big risk, to assume that Lila would change her mind. When I tried to talk with her more about it, she refused. "It's decided," Lila said. "It's not open for discussion."

I told Guthrie he ought to do something.

"Me?" Guthrie said. "Like what?"

"I don't know. She listens to you. Tell her she's got to come back."

"Why is this so important to you?" Guthrie asked.

"Because—because—" Good question. She could be really annoying, but she was my friend and I couldn't bear the thought of her leaving. I thought about all those awful times I'd had to leave a place, just when I was getting used to it. "Just because, Guthrie. Tell her she's got to come back."

Guthrie laughed. "It's not exactly my style,

Dinnie. Telling people what they've got to do is not exactly my thing."

"Talk to her, okay?"

"*Ecco!*" he said. "I will talk to the pistol."

I hounded Guthrie for days. "Did you talk to her yet? Did you?"

"Who?" Guthrie said.

"You know who—Lila."

"Oh yeah, the pistol. Yeah, I talked with her."

"Did you tell her she's got to come back?" I asked.

"No."

"Why not?"

Guthrie grinned. "We talk about other stuff. I didn't get around to ordering her what to do yet."

On the night before the last day of classes, I met Lila outside her dormitory. I asked her if she'd talked with Guthrie.

"Sure," she said. "Why?"

"About not coming back—did you talk with him about that?"

"Yes."

The air was brisk and cold and still. I felt as

if time were slowing, freezing. I was in my bubble and I was Dinnie the dot. "And—?"

Lila looked away, down over the hillside, toward the mountain opposite. She spoke in a monotone, as if she were reading the words off the side of the mountain. "He said he agreed with me. Guthrie said I shouldn't come back if I didn't want to. At least he understands how I feel. Guthrie said this was a strange place and it wasn't for everybody and some people couldn't make it here. I told him that it wasn't a matter of 'making it' here. I could make it here if I wanted to. I just don't want to."

"Did he tell you about the ski term? Did he tell you about St. Moritz?"

Lila let out a bored, tired sigh. "Yes, he told me, but he said I shouldn't come back just because of some old ski term. He said I might not like ski term anyway—"

Time wasn't freezing. Time was rushing, rushing past. It was being swallowed up, disappearing. "Not *like* it?" I said. "Everybody likes it. They love it. It's *fantastico*! Everybody says so. Everybody."

"Guthrie said I might not like it. He said it's

just a bunch of people racing down the mountains, and if you didn't like the people, you might not like being cooped up with them for two weeks in St. Moritz. I'm the kind of person who doesn't like being cooped up."

"Cooped up? You're not cooped up at St. Moritz. You're outside all day. Everybody says so. It's *fantastico*—it's—you're—"

Lila yawned. "Guthrie said a person really had to like adventure to like St. Moritz. I told him it wasn't a matter of my not liking adventure. I'm the kind of person who loves adventure. I just don't like *this* adventure."

St. Abbondio's bells rang once, twice, three times—

"Gotta go," Lila said. "Don't look so pitiful. I'll write."

19

∴ Buon Natale ∴

The Dreams of Domenica Santolina Doone

A long line of people were making their way along a narrow path. Bundles dropped off their backs and lay where they fell, tripping the people behind them. A baby fell off a mother's back and rolled to the edge of the path and on down the hillside, down, down, down.

On Christmas Eve, Uncle Max, Aunt Sandy and I walked down the Collina d'Oro through the snow to the church of St. Abbondio. Inside were red poinsettias and gold ribbons and hundreds of candles. Whole families were there together: great-grandparents and grandparents and parents and teenagers and toddlers and cherry-cheeked babies.

"*Buon Natale,*" people said to us, and we to them. "*Buon Natale!*"

Just before the service started, Mrs. Stirling appeared at the door. She was wearing a long black cape over her black dress and a black lace mantilla over her face. People turned to look at her. She looked regal, gliding down the aisle, pausing to touch the hands of people she knew. She slipped into our pew and sat beside me. "Isn't this beautiful?" she whispered.

After a group of boys and girls had sung a Christmas carol, Mrs. Stirling leaned toward me and, tapping her program, said, "Look at this, Domenica dear. *Voci bianche*—that's what we just heard. It means 'white voices.' Isn't that a lovely way to put it?"

She'd said it like this: *VO-chee bee-ON-kay.* White voices. I sat there thinking about what blue voices might be, and red ones, and violet ones. At the end of the program, we heard more white voices, more *voci bianche*, clear and pure, soaring up to the beamed ceiling, and I wished I could sing like they did.

In one school I'd been in, I'd joined the choir, but after a week of rehearsals the choir director asked me if I would please just mouth the words.

"Don't actually sing out loud," he said.

As I sat in the church of St. Abbondio listening to the *voci bianche*, I thought maybe I'd take singing lessons. It would be a good struggle for me. I would try really, really hard and the teacher would block his ears and wring his hands and pray to heaven, but at least my struggle might make me more interesting. People would say, "Look at that Dinnie, struggling away, trying to learn how to sing. Isn't she valiant?"

But in the end, I figured that struggling to learn how to sing was probably not a very important struggle in the scheme of things. Unless, perhaps, I was trying to be the soloist in an opera, and I was desperate to be the best singer ever in the whole world and . . .

"Domenica?" Mrs. Stirling said. "Domenica? We're leaving—"

We walked back up the hill with Mrs. Stirling, who insisted we join her at her house for a nightcap. We sat by the fireplace as she bustled about, thrusting silver bowls of nuts and candies at us, and dashing to the next room to answer the phone, which rang about every five minutes. She'd answer the phone, "*Pronto?*" in the Italian way, but then, depending on her caller, she'd switch to English or French or continue in Italian.

Aunt Sandy sat there shaking her head. "I don't know how she does it," she whispered. "I'm half her age, and I'm pooped."

We left to the tune of Mrs. Stirling's effusive *buon natales,* and Aunt Sandy and I stood on the walk as Mrs. Stirling kept Uncle Max behind for a few more minutes. We heard the words "fix" and "change," and he came away fishing in his pocket for a piece of paper on which to make notes.

On the way home, Aunt Sandy said, "I'm sure your parents sent you something, Dinnie. I'm sure they did, but with the mail you can never tell. It's probably held up somewhere."

A month earlier, I had sent a package to my family, of photographs that I'd taken and developed in photography class. When it came time to choose which photo was for which person, I realized that I had already chosen when I had taken the photos in the first place.

The photo of a man fishing, that was for my father. A woman at an easel beside Lake Lugano, that was for my mother. A young woman pushing a baby carriage, for Stella. A juggler entertaining toddlers, for the baby. A young man in a black leather jacket, for Crick.

My photography teacher had said, "Specializing in portraits? Interesting subjects you've chosen."

Only when I was wrapping them up did I see that I'd photographed my family, or substitutes for my family.

A week after I mailed the package, we got a card from my mother saying they were moving farther north in New Mexico, to Taos. She'd send an address when she knew it. I imagined my package sitting forlornly in the post office, or falling off a truck and rolling off the road and down a long hill.

"We'll call them on Christmas Day," Aunt Sandy had said.

"We don't know their new number," I said.

"We'll get it from Information, don't worry," Aunt Sandy said.

Their old phone was disconnected. There was no listing for them in Taos.

"I'm sure they're trying to call us this very

minute!" Aunt Sandy said. We waited around all day, not leaving the house even for a walk in the new snow, but there was no call.

Under the tree at Aunt Sandy and Uncle Max's were three small packages for me, and an envelope. In the packages were: ski gloves, ski goggles, and one of the "children" from the spider plant, which had been replanted in its own pot. In the envelope was a piece of paper on which they'd written: *Santa dropped something on the balcony: go see!*

I rushed to the balcony and pushed open the doors. There, propped against the railing was a shiny new pair of skis, and beneath them, a pair of ski boots.

"Go ahead," Aunt Sandy urged. "Bring them in. Try them on."

"They're for me?" I said.

"Of course they're for you," Uncle Max said.

"Dinnie?" Aunt Sandy said. "Don't cry—"

"I'm not crying." But I was. I could hardly touch the skis. I loved them, but I'd never received anything like that before. They were so grand, and I didn't deserve them, and I didn't want to be so greedy for them, but I was. I hoped my parents wouldn't find out that Aunt Sandy and Uncle Max had given me anything so expensive, but if they did find out, I hoped they wouldn't feel bad.

Aunt Sandy and Uncle Max made me bring the skis inside where I tried on the boots and then the skis, right there in the living room, and later that day I took them to my room and put them on again and held the poles and pretended I was skiing. And then I took them off and wiped off the few smudges they'd acquired and stood them in the closet, but I left the closet door open so I could admire them from my bed.

The next day we took the train up to Grindelwald, where the snow was deep and blindingly white. We watched a parade of Swiss in national costume, and cows with huge swinging bells, and everywhere people were speaking German, which still sounded like *achtenspit* and *flickenspit* to me. We took a horse-drawn sleigh through the village, and I was Dinnie the dot in my bubble, sealed up tight, but I was dreaming of my skis and wishing I'd brought them so I could try them out.

That night, back at home, I watered my new

spider plant. *How did it feel?* I wondered. Was it happy to have its roots in its own soil, or was it lonely, cut off from its mother?

I kept waking up throughout the night. I was uneasy about something, but I couldn't figure out what it was. And then I saw the skis. What was it about those skis?

At about four o'clock in the morning, this is what I decided: I hadn't had to struggle for those skis. Someone had given them to me out of their own generosity, without my having struggled for them, without my having earned them.

I thought maybe I should give them back and tell Aunt Sandy and Uncle Max that first I'd better earn the money for them. I'd wash floors and windows and chop wood and do all the laundry and all the cooking. What a struggle!

But in the end, I decided that it was Christmas and people liked to be generous at Christmas, and maybe I ought to just accept this struggle-free gift. It might be hard to do—wait! That would be my struggle. I would struggle to accept their generosity. Yes, I would.

I put a sign in my window: GRAZIE.

20

∴ Trees and Cows ∼

The week after Christmas, I received two letters, one from Crick and one from Aunt Tillie. Each was written before Christmas. Crick said:

> Hey Dinnie goober! Guess what? I'm not in jail, and I may have a new opportunity. I'll tell you about it when I find out for sure.
>
> Got our Christmas tree today. It was too big for the car, and it didn't fit the tree stand, and it fell over every ten minutes, until I tied it to the curtains. Then it pulled down the curtains. It's on the floor right now. Big mess. Gotta go fix it.
>
> Wish you were here,
> Your macho-macho brother,
> Crick

Aunt Tillie enclosed a copy of her Christmas letter. It was a month-by month outline of life on her farm. It went like this:

> *January:*
> *Baked strawberry cheesecake jello and milked cows.*
>
> *February:*
> *Baked peach cheesecake jello and milked cows.*
>
> *March:*
> *Baked apple cheesecake jello and milked cows.*
>
> *April:*
> *Baked blueberry cheesecake jello and milked cows.*

It went on like that through December. At the bottom, she had added this note:

> *Hi Dinnie darlin'——*
> *Grace gave me a copy of her Christmas letter to mail to you because she is too lazy to go to the post office and get some stamps, but I'm not mailing it to you because she didn't do nothing all year but make pot roast and it wasn't even very good pot roast even though she tries. Lord knows she tries.*
> *I hope people in Switzerland celebrate Christmas*

and that you have a wing-ding of a one even though
you won't be with your family, which is too bad.

I am sending you forty-two gazillion
kisses from me—

Your best Aunt—Tillie

21

⌁ Libero ⌁

The bus from Lugano had crossed the Julier pass, and from there to St. Moritz, the sun sparkling off the ten-foot-high snow drifts was so bright and sharp that it hurt your eyes. You wanted to stare out at the white, white mountains and valleys, but your eyes would water and you'd have to stare down at the dark floor of the bus to calm them.

The Hotel Laudinella squatted low in the valley of St. Moritz, midway between the *Signalbahn* cableway to the beginner and intermediate slopes, and the *funicolare* to the higher slopes of Corviglia and Piz Nair. The low buildings of St. Moritz curved around a frozen lake, and surrounding the town and the lake were snow-covered mountains.

I had come down from Lugano a day early with Uncle Max and Aunt Sandy and the faculty. They'd put me to work, helping them set up their office on the ground floor of the Hotel Laudinella, and checking the rooms, to be sure they were ready for the two hundred students about to descend on the hotel.

Uncle Max and Aunt Sandy went up to the slopes to talk with the Swiss ski instructors, to confirm arrangements for the next day's lessons, in which students and faculty would be divided according to ability, and mixed—students and teachers—into groups.

When they returned from the slopes, Aunt Sandy rushed into the school's makeshift office in the Laudinella, dressed in a red ski suit, her face flushed from the sharp, cold air. "Dinnie!" she said. "I've got to take you up there—you won't believe it! You can see for miles and miles and miles. You're on top of the world up there. This is going to be brilliant!"

Uncle Max looked less sure. He had just learned, from the school nurse, that during the previous year's ski term, there had been twelve fractures among the students.

"Twelve?" Uncle Max had said. "Twelve?"

"Not so bad," the nurse had said. "Some were

just thumbs, you know. Everyone falls on their thumbs sooner or later."

"And the others?" Uncle Max said.

"Oh, some normal ones. Legs, you know. A couple arms. And only two really bad ones— multiples—legs and arms. They've got a good hospital here. They're used to fractures."

"Are you going to be able to enjoy this?" Aunt Sandy asked him.

Uncle Max slumped into a chair. "I don't know. Trying to move a whole school to a hotel? The idea of two hundred students zinging down a mountain? I don't know about this."

I hovered near the fax machine. A steady stream of paper rolled out of it. A flight from Tokyo was a day late. Nils and Hans were stuck in an Amsterdam airport. Fadi was ill and would be returning a week later. Pedro's lost luggage had been located and was on its way.

"Nothing about Lila?" I asked the school's receptionist.

"Lila-the-pistol?" she said. "No, nothing from Lila-the-pistol."

The first bus pulled up outside the Laudinella.

A clamor of boots and shouts poured out of it.

"Get ready," Aunt Sandy told Uncle Max. "Here they come—"

Luggage and skis were piled outside. Students scrambled to claim their belongings and clattered inside to get their room assignments.

"Hey, Dinnie!" Keisuke called.

Belen was behind him. "Dinnie! We made it!"

And then a whirlwind as students called to each other: "Gustav! Here! We're in with Marco and Faisal!"

"Sonal—Sonal—you're with me!"

"Where's Paulo? Seen Paulo?"

"Gherardo! Over here! We're with Yoichi and Tim!"

"Nadya! Kelly! We're together!"

And there was Guthrie, with that wide grin. "Hey, Dinnie!" he called. "Want to help me with this stuff? Isn't this the best? Don't you love this place? Man, I can't wait to get out on that mountain! It's going to be brilliant! We're going to have the best time you ever saw in your whole life. Hey, Keisuke! Over here! You're with me—"

"Seen Lila?" I asked Guthrie.

"Who? Lila? Haven't seen her. She's probably on one of the other buses. Man! We've got to get up that mountain. Where's your gear?"

"I don't know how to ski," I said.

"What? You've never been down a mountain? You'll learn in no time. Then we'll go up to the top and whiz down together. But come on, at least come up with us while we get in a couple runs—"

"But—"

"You can sit in the café midway up. You can watch."

"Maybe I ought to stay around here and wait for Lila."

Keisuke said, "No way, you come on mountain. You come with us."

Guthrie threw me his jacket. "Got some goggles or something? It's going to be bright up there."

Outside it was bitter, bitter cold, but the sun shone bright and strong on the white snow, and if I kept moving and turned my face to the sun and pulled my knit hat down over my ears and my collar up over my neck, I could will myself to be warm inside all the layers. Guthrie and Keisuke led the way through the village to the bottom of the slope where we watched the *Signalbahn* swing high in the air and slide down to the platform.

I was scared, thinking of riding up the mountain in the *Signalbahn*. I had to shut off my mind, make it numb, and not think about being suspended in the air hundreds of feet above the snow, zooming up and up and up the mountain.

Guthrie and Keisuke and I were pushed along with the crowd of other skiers into the cable car, and then the doors closed and there was a jerk and *whoosh* as it left the platform and lifted into the air. I moved away from the window, burrowing into the middle of the crowd, staring down at the boots and the puddles of water where snow was melting.

I knelt to the floor, pretending to fix my boot, sick and queasy, knowing I was about to die. The cable would snap and we would fall, fall, fall—

There was a tremendous lurch and surge—this was it. The cable had broken! I heard others squeal. The car swung forward.

But it was only the halfway point, and we

weren't falling. "It always does that," I heard Guthrie telling someone else. *"Fantastico!"*

And at last the car slid to a quiet stop and I stood and was pushed out onto the platform with the others, and when I turned to look back, I had to grab for a pole because there it was—the long, long, long stretch down the mountain. You could see all of St. Moritz, a tiny speck now in the valley far below. And you could see beyond, over other mountains, and everywhere you looked it was white, white, white. Behind and above us was more mountain, rising higher, higher, and the sky was so blue, and the sun was a perfect round brilliant yellow circle overhead.

Guthrie grabbed my shoulder. "Isn't it the best? Isn't it magnificent?"

Just beyond the platform was an outdoor café. "You can sit here," Guthrie said. "You can watch. We're going to that lift—see there? And on up there." He waved his gloved hand farther up the mountain. "And then you'll see us zoom right down over there! Man, I feel free! Free! *Libero!*"

Guthrie and Keisuke sang and whooped all the way down from the top to the café, over and over. "*Sono libero!*" Guthrie shouted. "*Libero, libero, libero!*" They'd ski down to where I was, shout and laugh, and then ski straight back to the lift and on up they would go again.

"Look at this," Guthrie said once. "Look at it. It's God's country. It's our country! All ours for two whole weeks." He flexed his arms. "Power! *Sono potente!*"

I wanted to feel *potente*, too, like Guthrie, and for a moment there, as I watched him, I felt as if my little dot self was expanding. Guthrie and Keisuke took off again for the ski lift, and I laughed and laughed, and people turned to look at me, an expanding dot laughing to herself on the mountainside.

Keisuke and Guthrie raced and tumbled and flew down the mountain. Belen joined them, shouting and whooping. "*Viva* St. Moritz!"

We had lunch together in the café. "You've got to try this *raclette* stuff," Guthrie said. "*Viva raclette!*"

I stared at the *raclette*: potatoes and pickles swimming in a sea of melted cheese. "I wonder who thought of this combination," I said.

"God did!" Guthrie said. "It's the best. Such the best!" He'd already said this about the ski lifts, the snow, the views, the runs down the mountain. "Dinnie," he said, "I want you to bury me on this mountain. Those are my final wishes. Keisuke? Belen? Bear witness. When I die, Dinnie has to drag my body up here and bury me on this mountain."

"*Stew-pod,*" Keisuke said. "Ashes more easier."

"Okay, fine," Guthrie agreed. "If you don't want to drag my body up here, Dinnie, my ashes will do. Scatter them when you're skiing down the mountain. Like this—" He swung his arm across the table. "A little of me here, a little of me there—"

"*Demente,*" Belen said. "You have crazy brain."

"You know what it feels like when I'm up here on this mountain?" Guthrie asked. "It feels like— like angels are flying all around in my head!"

"Completely *demente,*" Belen said. "*Loco.*"

"*Stew-pod,*" Keisuke said.

22

~: St. Moritz :~

Back at the Hotel Laudinella, I headed straight for the school's office. Uncle Max was standing just inside the doorway.

"No Lila yet," he said. "Sorry."

"No fax? No call?" I said.

"Nothing yet."

I was rooming with Belen and another girl, Mari. Lila's name was also on the roster for our room, but none of us expected her to show up.

"Too bad," Mari said. "I was looking for a good dose of complaining."

Belen, to my surprise, said, "She's not so bad, that Lila. You just have to stay out of her way."

This was new for me, boarding with the students. Back in Lugano, where I had my own room at Uncle Max and Aunt Sandy's, I was often glad for the silence when I'd leave school and go home. But sometimes at school, when the others were talking about something that had happened in the

135

dorm the night before, or when they seemed as if they were sharing secrets exchanged in the late hours, I felt excluded from a secret society.

Now, in the Hotel Laudinella, I was watching, listening, trying to pick up the routine. At ten o'clock, Signora Palermo, the teacher in residence on our floor, knocked on our door to see that we were accounted for.

"No Lila?" she said. "Seven thousand demerits! I joke, yes?"

By ten-thirty, I'd brushed my teeth and gotten in bed.

"In bed already?" Mari said.

"I thought lights-out were at ten-thirty."

She and Belen laughed. "Watch," Mari said. She put a towel under the door. "Presto! Lights out!"

Belen showed us pictures that Keisuke had brought back for her. There was his house near Osaka, and his parents, his sister. There was Keisuke at home, Keisuke on the subway, Keisuke using chopsticks.

Mari asked Belen if she'd talked to Keisuke over the holiday.

"What, are you crazy?" Belen said. "My parents would shoot me if they knew about Keisuke!"

"Why?" I asked.

"He's Japanese, that's why. They want for me a nice Spanish boy."

Mari giggled. "Like Gherardo. Or Pablo. Or Manuel—"

Belen made a face. "No Manuel, please no Manuel! He eats like pig!"

Mari said, "My parents are the same. They expect for me to talk only about Italian boys. If I mention Fadi—"

"Ooh, Fadi!" Belen teased.

"If I mention Fadi, they say, 'Is that girl or boy? Better not be boy you talk about!'"

"What about you, Dinnie?" Belen said. She was sitting on the floor, leaning against my bed. "Who do you like?"

"No one in particular," I said.

"Not Guthrie?" Belen asked.

"Guthrie!" Mari said. "Guthrie? I thought Lila had him staked out—"

"Lila?" I said. "And Guthrie?" I don't know

why it hadn't occurred to me. Is that what people thought, that Lila and Guthrie were a couple?

There was a knock at the door.

"Are we in trouble?" I asked.

Belen threw her pillow at me and answered the door. It was Aunt Sandy. She didn't seem surprised or bothered that our lights were on.

"You all okay in here?" she asked.

"Any word?" I asked her. "About Lila?"

"Not yet. You girls need anything?"

"Sure," Belen said. "I need my Keisuke."

"A bottle of wine, Signora?" Mari joked.

"Very funny," Aunt Sandy said. I was surprised that they would joke with her like this, and that she seemed so at ease with them. Aunt Sandy had done loads of nighttime check-ins at school, but I'd never actually pictured her doing that before.

"And you, Dinnie?" Aunt Sandy asked. "You need anything?"

Belen and Mari said, "Guthrie! Bring her Guthrie!"

"That's the most ridiculous thing I ever heard!" I said.

"*Stew-pod?*" Belen said. "Is it *stew-pod?*"

After Aunt Sandy left, Mari and Belen talked on. They talked about what they got for Christmas and about their friends back home and about clothes and makeup.

"You know what makeup is called in Italian?" Mari said. "*Trucco!* It means *trick!* Don't you think that's funny?"

They told me they liked Uncle Max, that he was "a good guy." And then Belen remembered something Uncle Max had said in an assembly once. "Remember after Bork was expelled and your uncle gave that talk? Remember? He asked us that question: *What would you do if you knew you wouldn't be caught?* What a question! And didn't he say you could judge a person by what he would do if he knew he wouldn't get caught? I think about that all the time."

And so she and Mari talked about what they might do if they knew they wouldn't get caught. Would they steal a wallet? A television? Would they sneak out of the dorm? Would they kill someone?

•　•　•

The Dreams of Domenica Santolina Doone

I was running through the snow with my box of things, and I kept looking behind me to see if someone was chasing me. The box was taped up tight and there was a word written in black marker on the side: GUTHRIE. I had stolen Guthrie.

Twelve inches of snow fell overnight. I awoke to the sounds of booms: *Boom! Boom-boom-boom!*

"Military practice? At St. Moritz?" I said.

"That's not military practice," Mari said. "It's anti-avalanche stuff. Detonation."

"We're going up there? Where they're blowing up the mountain? Trying to set off avalanches? Trying to kill us?"

"Oh, Dinnie. It's to *prevent* an avalanche. They toss some dynamite or something up there to loosen the snow so it tumbles down before it all piles up into a big dangerous lump. Something like that. They'll be finished by the time we get up there."

The sky was clear by ten o'clock in the morning when we assembled on the mountain to split into ski groups. The sun beat down on the snow, and I took deep breaths. The air was different here. It was clear and thin and made me dizzy. Above was pure blue, and below was white, white, all the way down to the dots of brown chalets in the town below. In the distance, mountains lapped mountains as far as I could see.

When we'd boarded the *Signalbahn* below, a red sign was flashing, displaying words in German, then French, then Italian, and finally English: *AVALANCHE WARNING*. Uncle Max huddled with the ski instructors. "No, no," they said. "No worries. It's on the other side. We'll tell the kids not to ski off the posted runs. It will be fine."

I was terrified and woozy. I didn't want to go up the mountain, and I didn't want to ski down it.

Guthrie and Keisuke were in the most advanced ski class. I was standing with the beginners. Some in my group had put their skis on already and were sliding and falling, crashing into each other. There were ten students in our group, two teachers, and the ski instructor, whose name was Simone. In the distance, I saw Aunt Sandy in another beginner's group. She was laughing and brushing snow off her arms.

Simone said we were going to do a few exercises and learn how to put our skis on and take them off and how to fall. *You could learn how to fall?* Maybe I wouldn't faint right there on the mountain before the lesson began. Maybe I'd live through it.

In the distance, Guthrie's group was skiing toward the chair lift. They swished across the snow like skiers you see in movies. It looked so easy. A girl in a bright-pink ski jacket skied up behind Guthrie. Lila? Was it Lila? I called to her, "Li-la!" She turned vaguely toward me, but didn't see me waving my ski poles. "Hey, Guthrie! Lila!" I called, but my shout bounced back to me and rolled on down the mountain.

23

~: Downfelling :~

L ila was back, and she was different. She smiled and laughed, she embraced everyone she met, and she seemed bent on meeting everyone she didn't already know. She was a regular walking, talking Miss Personality.

Everything was "marvelous" and "brilliant." Everyone was "terrific." Switzerland was *fantastico*.

At first, people said, "What happened to the pistol?" and "Did she get a brain transplant or what?" But that didn't last long. If you were going to make a new start, there probably wasn't a better place to do it than in St. Moritz, where each day's new snow made the world seem like a clean canvas, and where, at the end of the day, your body was too tired and too full of fresh air to be cynical.

That's the way my body felt, at least. My body was a pitiful mass of aching muscles. Everything hurt: my legs, my feet, my arms, my hands, my neck, my back. Even my eyeballs hurt.

I had learned how to fall, and I did it frequently. I toppled putting on my skis and taking them off. I tumbled trying to get on the T-bar and trying to get off it. I'd get fifteen feet down the mountain, braced in snowplow position, lurching about one inch a minute, and I'd sprawl, a tangle of skis and poles.

I was a really good fall-er, a champion falling person. I could fall on my back or my right side or my left. I could flop on my face or on my ear. I could pitch forward onto my stomach. I could—and did—fall in every position you could imagine.

When Guthrie and Keisuke and Belen and Lila and I would meet up at the café for lunch, I'd be a scraggly mess, with snow melting in every crevice of my clothing, snow in my hair and my ears, my ski suit ripped or torn in some new place. I'd be minus a glove or my goggles. My ski poles were bent into contorted shapes, and my skis looked as if I'd battered them against a rock.

"You do much downfelling," Keisuke said.

But they all looked glamorous. Their cheeks

were tanned, their clothes dry, their poles and skis and boots intact. I'd clatter in saying, "I think I'm gonna die. I know I'm gonna die," and they'd be sitting there sipping hot chocolate, talking about the great run they'd just had and what a marvelous, *fantastico* day it was.

"Don't you just *love* this place?" Lila asked me one day. "Isn't it *such* the best? Isn't it *fantastico*?"

I wanted to slug her. "It's *stew-pod*," I said. "Completely *stew-pod*."

But it wasn't *stew-pod*, not really. I liked the abbreviated academic classes in the morning, and the fresh air all day. I liked coming back to the hotel and sinking into a hot tub and then scurrying on to the remainder of the academic classes and then scomfing down dinner and lazily staring at my books during the shortened study hall and then collapsing into my bed each night. And by the second week, I'd gone all the way down the beginner slope without *downfelling* once, and I'd even managed to do it without snow-plowing the whole way down. I, Domenica Santolina Doone, was a skier!

• • •

· ·

The Dreams of Domenica Santolina Doone

I leaped off the chair lift into the new snow and skied down a mountain and even up a mountain and down again. I leaped over a wide, wide crevice and sailed down the mountain and zipped around moguls, and at the bottom, everyone cheered. I won. I don't know what I won because I woke up.

· ·

24

~: Disaster :~

Too soon the two weeks were over and we were back in Lugano, and there we learned about Disaster.

We weren't completely ignorant. We knew about disaster from our previous schools and previous lives. We'd had access to televisions and newspapers. But the return to Lugano marked the beginning of Global Awareness Month, and in each of our classes, we talked about disaster: disaster man-made and natural. We talked about ozone depletion and the extinction of species and depleted rain forests and war and poverty and AIDS. We talked about refugees and slaughter and famine.

We were in the middle school and were getting, according to Uncle Max, a diluted version of what the upper-schoolers were facing. An Iraqi boy from the upper school came to our history class and talked about what it felt like when the Americans bombed his country. Keisuke talked about how he felt responsible for World War II, and a German student said she felt the same.

We got into heated discussions over the neglect of infant females in some cultures, and horrific cases of child abuse worldwide. We fasted one day each week to raise our consciousness about hunger, and we sent money and canned goods and clothing to charities.

In one class, after we watched a movie about traumas in Rwanda, and a Rwandan student told us about seeing his mother killed, Mari threw up. We were all having nightmares.

At home, Aunt Sandy pleaded with Uncle Max. "This is too much!" she said. "You can't dump all the world's problems on these kids in one lump!"

And he agreed. He was bewildered by it all, but the program had been set up the previous year, and he was the new headmaster, reluctant to interfere. And though we were sick of it and about it, we were greedy for it. We felt privileged there in our protected world and we felt guilty, and this was our punishment.

It took the wind out of Guthrie. He slumped along, muttering to himself. "What are we going to do, Dinnie?" he'd say to me. "What can we do? We've got to do *something!*"

He talked about leaving school and going to war-torn Rwanda to help. "You're too young," someone told him. "You wouldn't get across the border."

He wrote to the American president and the Swiss ambassador. He joined Greenpeace and Amnesty International. He started an after-school discussion group called UP—Unite for Peace. After a week of that, he said, "It's awful. It's just talk, talk, talk. Talk gets nowhere. People are *dying*, Dinnie, they're dying all around us, everywhere. People are starving and sick and they're being murdered and tortured."

I knew it. I thought of it day and night. One night, after a recurring nightmare about refugees, I woke Uncle Max up. "What are you doing here? Why aren't you helping the refugees? Why did you bring me here? Who's paying for me to be here?"

Aunt Sandy woke in the middle of my tirade and said, "Dinnie?"

I had a sudden recollection of something that had happened one Thanksgiving in Oklahoma. At my school, we'd been asked to bring in canned goods for "needy families." The school was going to assemble boxes for these families, and the county was donating turkeys for them, too.

The teacher said that anyone who wanted to volunteer to go along and help distribute these items on Saturday should meet in the parking lot, where other community volunteers would meet us.

I went there on that Saturday and joined two of my classmates in a car with a woman named Mrs. Burke. She was very cheery. "Okay!" she said. "I have a list here and the addresses, so here we go!" And for the next few hours, we distributed boxes to families in rundown houses. Some of the families were very happy to see us, but some were not, and I couldn't understand why. One man refused to accept the box and chased us out of his yard.

"Okay!" Mrs. Burke said. "Two more to go.

Let me check my list. One's out on Colby Road—we'll go there first."

"I live on that road, too!" I said, and I wondered what family we'd be visiting.

"Wonderful!" Mrs. Burke said. "Then you can show me the way if I get lost!"

We drove out into the countryside and she found Colby Road without any trouble, and as we were driving along, she looked at her list again and said, "Okay! Now we've got to look for 499—"

"But—" I said.

"We must be close," Mrs. Burke said. "That's 455—"

"But—"

And then she was pulling into my drive, and I was dying, dying a thousand deaths. I sat there, frozen, as Mrs. Burke and my classmates hopped out and and took a box from the trunk and started for the house.

My mother opened the door and had such a puzzled look on her face. She glanced toward the car and saw me sitting there, frozen, and then she smiled at Mrs. Burke and took the box and thanked her, and then I got out of the car and said to Mrs. Burke, "I live here. Am I done now?"

Mrs. Burke turned very red and put her hand to her mouth and leaned down and said, "Oh, honey, thank you for coming with me, I'm sorry if—I didn't know—I wouldn't have—"

"It's okay," I said, and I went inside and my mother was staring at the box of food and she said, "Dinnie, we are grateful to have this food right now, and you did a nice thing today, so don't you feel bad about it."

But I did feel bad about it and I didn't want to go back to my school, and fortunately for me, my father found a new opportunity somewhere else, and so a month later we were gone.

I was thinking of all that as I stood in Aunt Sandy and Uncle Max's bedroom that night, and I said, "I'm a charity case, aren't I? I don't belong here. I should be with the refugees. You should, too."

Uncle Max went and made a pot of coffee, and when he returned he said, "Dinnie, kids here have problems, too. You don't see them, but they're there. They need someone to help them, too."

"Who's paying for me?"

"Not everyone here is rich, Dinnie. There are lots of students on financial aid, and lots of students are here because their parents' companies pay for them to attend."

"Who?" I said. "Name some."

"I can't do that," Uncle Max said. "And besides, what difference does it make?"

"I just want to know."

"Dinnie," Aunt Sandy said. "You're here because Uncle Max is the headmaster. It's like a bonus in his job. You get to attend. No one has to pay. It's a privilege. You're *lucky*."

"I don't want to be a lucky one. I should be suffering, like the refugees."

Uncle Max looked bewildered. "Why, Dinnie, why? You're allowed to be lucky. Maybe one day you can make someone else lucky."

"It's an *opportunity*, Dinnie," Aunt Sandy said.

Oh, that old word, it rumbled around in my head, round and round and round.

"And," Aunt Sandy said, "it's your choice. You

can either take advantage of the opportunity—
or not. It's up to you."

I thrashed around all night long, feeling miser-
able. Here I had all these opportunities, while the
refugees had none. I wanted to give them everything. "Here," I would say to them. "Take them.
Take Switzerland and the mountains, the church
bells, the skis. Take them all. You deserve them."

But I didn't know how to find the refugees and
how to give them Switzerland.

. . . .

The Dreams of Domenica Santolina Doone

*I was in my room at Uncle Max and Aunt Sandy's
house, and I looked out the window and saw my family
climbing up the hill: my mother, my father, Crick, and Stella,
carrying her baby. They were barefoot and their clothes were
torn.*

*When they came in the house, my mother tried on my
ski jacket and Crick ran his hands over my skis. Stella
said, "Is this all yours, Dinnie?" and I said, "No!" and
then I pulled out my old box of things and said, "See?
Only this is mine," but when I opened the box, all kinds*

of new things were in it: a radio and ski boots and gloves
and hats and sweaters and jewelry, and then my father
and mother and Crick and Stella and the baby climbed
out the window and left.
. . . .

Global Awareness Month surged on. Lila went
mute. Her new "amazing" and "incredible" and
"fantastico" self was silenced. In classes and in the
dorms, all around her, she heard people complaining, just as she had used to do, but they were
complaining about real trauma. She couldn't
revert to complaining about the food, because
people were afraid to eat it, thinking of all the
starving humanity, all the millions of starving
people in the world.

Three weeks into Global Awareness Month,
Uncle Max stepped in. He made a speech about
the necessity of being globally aware, but he said
our job was to educate ourselves so that when we
were adults, we would make informed decisions.
He said that we not only needed to know about
disaster, but we needed to know about the spirit,
too. We needed to know about art and beauty and

music and laughter, so that we could change the world.

It helped. We didn't all buy it, but it helped. After Uncle Max's speech, I saw Guthrie standing on the villa balcony, looking down over the lake. He was crying.

. . . .

The Dreams of Domenica Santolina Doone

I was sitting in a chair in my bubble ball on top of a hill, looking down on a long, long line of refugees weaving in and out of the narrow paths below. Children were scream-ing. Soldiers barreled down the hill shooting their guns. Acid rain fell on their heads, and the trees fell over, crashing into the people and disintegrating in a cloud of black dust.

I rolled down the hill and started passing things through my bubble to the refugees. I gave them church bells and skis and even a whole mountain.

The rain was pecking at my bubble, eating its way through, and when a drop fell, sharp and stinging, onto my forehead, I woke up and saw a mosquito buzzing above me.

. . . .

25

~: Phone Call :~

At the end of February, the Christmas package from my parents finally arrived. The box looked as if cows had trampled over it and munched the corners. Inside was a small photo album, which I opened eagerly, excited at the thought of seeing pictures of my family. But there were no photos inside. Tucked in the front was one of my mother's paintings on which she had written *Dinnie Fishing*. It showed a girl standing on the bank of a river, holding a fishing net. There was an empty space in the blue sky—a ragged brown splotch—and in the net was the sun.

On the next page, my mother had written this note: *Dinnie: A place to keep a record of all your adventures there in Switzerland. . . .*

The rest of the album was blank.

Also in the package were two cards. One was signed *Mom* and *Dad*. They had each written their own signatures. The other card was signed in Stella's handwriting: *Love from Stella, George, and Michael.*

George? Michael? Who were they? And then I remembered that the baby was Michael, and George was the name of her Marine husband.

A week later, another package arrived. In it was a red hand-knitted scarf, and a note from Grandma Fiorelli:

> *Domenica, carissima,*
> *Buon Natale. Adesso non ti raffredi piu.*
> *Nonna*

She'd said: *Merry Christmas. Now you won't be cold anymore.*

The day after her package arrived, my parents phoned. Their voices were clear but strange because I wasn't used to hearing them. I kept pressing the phone harder and harder against my ear, as if I could slip into the phone and down the wire and be there in the same room with them. There was a delay in the transmission, so that we'd start talking at the same time and would end up saying, "What? No, you—you go ahead," and "I—what? What'd you say? No, you—go ahead."

They took turns on the phone. They said they had a timer set, because it was very expensive to call all the way to Switzerland. Each one could talk for three minutes; that's what they had agreed. We were each asking questions a mile a minute, and there wasn't time to answer the questions.

I did find out that they were in Taos. Dad had a great opportunity there, he said. Stella was back in school, and Mom was watching the baby in the mornings, and a neighbor was watching the baby in the afternoons until Stella got home.

"Crick?" I kept asking. "Where's Crick?"

They'd say, "What? No, you—you go ahead, what'd you say?"

"Crick? Where is he?"

Finally, they told me he was in the Air Force. A judge had given him a choice. He could go to jail or he could sign up for military duty.

Dad said, "The Air Force will be good for him. It's a great opportunity! He can start all over!"

I asked him if he knew where Grandma

Fiorelli had lived in Italy, before she came to America. I should have asked my mother, because Grandma Fiorelli was her mother, but my mother's turn on the phone was done, and I'd forgotten to ask her. When I asked my father where Grandma Fiorelli had lived, he said, "Why do you want to know that?"

In the background I heard my mother say, "What? What does she want to know?"

My father told my mother, "Nothing. Never mind." I heard the *ding* of a timer, and he said, "Time's up! Be good—" There was a crackle in his voice, and he added, "We love you, Dinnie."

My mother grabbed the phone and said, "We do, we do, 'bye, Dinnie, 'bye—"

There was a click and a buzz and then silence. To the silent phone, I said, "I love you, too. I miss you and I love you and I haven't forgotten you and I miss you and I—"

"It's okay, Dinnie," Aunt Sandy said, replacing the receiver. "It's okay."

That night I consulted my Italian dictionary and put a new sign in my window: *LOTTANTE*.

When Aunt Sandy came in, she said, "What's

that mean? Doesn't it mean *struggling*? Is that what you meant?"

"Yep," I said.

She patted the top of my head. "I know, honey, I know." She tapped my pillow. "If you want to talk about anything, let us know, okay?"

"Okay," I said.

. . . .

The Dreams of Domenica Santolina Doone

I was standing on Mt. San Salvatore, and a plane, slim as a black bullet, went over. Crick was the pilot. I was holding a sign that said DON'T BOMB ANYONE! but after the plane was gone, I realized that I'd written it in Italian, and Crick couldn't read Italian.

. . . .

26

∴ Hamburger and Peaches :∼

Two more cards arrived from Aunt Grace
and Aunt Tillie:

Dear Dinnie,

 Did Tillie ever send you my Christmas
letter? You didn't mention it. I bet she forgot to
send it. She'd forget her head if it wasn't stuck on
her neck.

 My bum knee is still bum, but Lonnie got me a
cane. I'm turning into an old lady.

 When are you coming home? Don't turn into a
Switz, okay?

 I'm making hamburger-peach casserole tonight.
It was in a magazine.

 Love, love, love,

 Your Aunt Grace

Dear Dinnie,

I got a letter from you and your daddy on the same day, isn't that something? He is worrying over you, and missing you, like always.

I heard about Crick. Don't fret. The Air Force won't put up with any shenanigans from him, so he'll have to do some real work for a change. It won't kill him. He's a good boy, I know it.

I was walking by the river the other day, and I was thinking about you. I think I might do a spell of fishing myself.

Guess what your Aunt Grace is making for dinner tonight?? (I'm invited.) Hamburger-peach casserole! Lord have mercy! Maybe I won't chew.

Two truckloads of kisses,

Love from your Aunt Tillie, Champion Cheesecake Jello Maker

I also received a postcard from my mother, which arrived six weeks after she'd sent it because she had the address wrong. Instead of *Via Poporino* she'd written *Via Popcorn*, and instead of *Montagnola*, she'd written *Mount Holy*. Her card said:

Dear Dinnie:

   We are in Taos and it is beautiful.

   Beneath that, she'd drawn a picture of a mountain, with a little cabin hanging off the side of it.

27

~: Italian Invasion :~

By March, Italian was taking over my brain. In my dreams I was not only jabbering away in Italian, but I was also thinking in Italian while I was watching my dream-self jabber. In my dreams, I didn't stumble over words. I barreled on; I pulled Italian words from the air.

But in my waking life, in Italian class, I was not so proficient. Words would come out of my mouth and Signora Palermo would look at me as if I were speaking Arabic. "Mm," she'd say. *"Puoi ripetere, per favore,"* and so I'd repeat and new words would come out, some right, some wrong. "It sounds like it *ought* to be Italian," she'd say, "but I think you've thrown some Japanese in there." The Japanese I'd picked up from Keisuke and his friends, but I'd say the Japanese words with an Italian accent. My Italian tongue was taking charge.

Since I hadn't yet mastered the past tense, I was limited in what I could say. I could talk about today and now, but I couldn't talk about yesterday or last week or month or year. I'd end up saying things that, when translated, went something like *I eat a pizza yesterday* or *I buy this shirt last month but it does not fit and I take it back last week.* It was like being snagged on a rock in a river: I couldn't go back, and I couldn't go around the next bend. I was just flopping there in the right-now middle.

Words I'd hear in English, I'd automatically be converting into Italian in my head. At home, Uncle Max and Aunt Sandy and I spoke a hodge-podge of English and Italian. "Pass the *latte, per favore*" and "Have you seen my *giacca*?"

Guthrie thought I understood more Italian than I did. He'd yammer away in Italian, and I'd catch about four words out of ten, and I'd mumble, "*Si, si,*" or, if it looked like he were telling me something I should be surprised about, I'd use my favorite phrase, "*Non é vero!*" (*No such thing!* or *Not true!*). It made me feel very cool to say *Non é vero!*

I threw my hands around a lot in extravagant

gestures, which is what Guthrie did and what the locals did. What you said sounded more Italian if you sliced the air with your hands as you were saying it. Your whole body could help the words—the flip of your hands, the jerk of your head, the crossing of your legs.

At the end of March, my mother sent me a postcard with one line on it:

Your grandparents were born in Campobasso,
Italy.

Aunt Sandy saw the card and said, "Were they really? My own parents, and I didn't know where they were born! Shameful!"

Campobasso, Campobasso. I couldn't find it on the map in my Italian classroom. Signora Palermo said she'd never heard of it, "but it means low ground. Campobasso must be a low flat place," she said.

"I'm going to go there," I told Signora Palermo.

"Oh?" she said. *"Quando?"* (When?)

I gave my best Italian shrug and said, *"Una*

zanzara." I thought I was saying *some day*, but she informed me that I'd just said *a mosquito*. I'm not sure where that mosquito came from.

By March, we'd all become used to Mr. (Cuckoo) Koo, the science teacher, too. If you'd asked me which I preferred: a teacher who said encouraging things like "Nice job" and "Great improvement!" or a teacher like Mr. Koo who said things like "You beanhead, read that chapter again!," I'd have chosen the encouraging teacher any day. But there was always a frizzle of excitement as we entered Mr. Koo's class. What was he going to say today? And since he doled out his insults to everyone in turn and didn't have any pets, it was easier to take it when he zeroed in on you. Afterward, your classmates would be very sympathetic.

We did learn a lot. We were afraid *not* to learn.

"Okay, Mr. Exuberance Guthrie, stand up and explain the difference between a tropical rain forest and a jungle. Up, up, up! Stand up, stand straight!"

Guthrie was smiling. He knew the answer.

"Well—"

"I'm not asking you about wells," Mr. Koo said. "Did I say anything about wells?"

Guthrie began again. "A jungle is usually found by rivers—"

"By rivers? You mean on the riverbanks?

"Yes."

"Then say 'riverbanks,' don't mumble along saying things you don't mean, sharpen up that vocabulary, and straighten your tie."

Guthrie straightened his tie. "A jungle might become a rain forest—"

"And what is a rain forest then, come on, we don't have all day, speed it up, don't be a bean-head—"

It was in March, too, that our English teacher got radical. Mr. Bonner said we'd had too much homework, too many essays, and so we'd have no written homework for a month. (Aunt Sandy said he was probably just tired of grading essays.) Mr. Bonner also announced that we'd have no reading homework either. In class, we were going to read *Romeo and Juliet* (the boys groaned), but outside of class, our homework was "to think."

"That's all?" Belen asked. "Only think?"

"'Only?'" he said. "Thinking is the hardest thing of all."

Keisuke said, "So how you grade? How you grade thinking?"

"Very good question. Very good indeed. So that will be the first homework. Think about how we could grade thinking."

Everyone looked as if he'd asked us to solve a ten-page mathematical equation. Mari leaned over to me and said, "Do you think he's drunk or something?"

He passed out copies of *Romeo and Juliet* and said it was a story about two people our age who were in love, but their parents were enemies, and so they couldn't be together. Belen and Keisuke stared at each other. Guthrie whispered, "It's about *them*! It's about Keisuke and Belen!"

Keisuke opened his book. "This English?" he said. "I understand nothing."

Mr. Bonner said, "Don't worry about the words right now." He asked us to imagine two families, fairly well-off, living in the city of

Verona in Italy. (I wondered if Verona was near Campobasso.) "Or anywhere," he said. "You could imagine these two families anywhere you want: in Germany, in Japan, in France, in Spain—"

After class, Guthrie said, "Hey, Keisuke! Brilliant! We're going to read about you and Belen!"

"Shut up," Belen said. "Mr. Bonner said this play's a *tragedy*. I want no more hearing about tragedies."

"Why can't we read comedy or something?" Keisuke added. "Why always people dying dead?"

Guthrie stared at his feet. "Because that's what happens. All the time. Every day." He slung his book bag over one shoulder and waved at the sky. "But *guardate*! Sun! Anyone signed up for skiing this weekend? Let's all go—there's a trip up to Andermatt. Let's go! We'll conquer the mountains! It'll be such the best!"

28

~: Thinking :~

I thought we'd probably discuss "how to grade thinking" for about two minutes. Instead, we discussed it in class for three days. Our discussions began very civilized, with people suggesting that we could write down what we think and the teacher could grade it, but then people said if we had to write it down, it was written homework, and besides, how was the teacher going to grade the thinking? What was *good* thinking and what was *bad* thinking?

By the second day, discussion had erupted into heated arguments. The teacher was American, so wouldn't he favor American thinking? Why was American thinking better than Korean thinking? Mari nearly punched Keisuke when he suggested that Japanese think more clearly than Italians. "Japanese think with head," he said. "Italians think with foot. No, no, I mean heart."

"That's *stew-pod*," Mari said.

By the third day, we'd all come to the same conclusion: You could probably grade thinking, but it wouldn't necessarily be fair grading, so we proposed that thinking should not be graded at all.

"Fine with me," Mr. Bonner said.

"Fine? You agree?" Mari said. "We can think whatever we want?"

It seemed a revelation. Daring. I didn't tell Uncle Max about this new plan of Mr. Bonner's, because I was afraid he might fire Mr. Bonner.

Sometimes Mr. Bonner suggested the topic for the thinking homework, and sometimes students did. If we wanted another night or two to think about something, we got it. Usually one thinking question led to another one, and another and another.

"It's brilliant," Guthrie said. "Absolutely brilliant."

Most of the thinking questions seemed to pop up while we were reading *Romeo and Juliet*. These are some of the things we thought about:

Is it better to choose your own spouse or have an arranged marriage?

I thought everyone would say it was better to

choose your own, but there were students in the class, like Fadi, who were from cultures where arranged marriages were common. Fadi made it sound so reasonable, so practical, to have someone else choose your mate. Then everyone started switching sides. Those who first thought it was better to choose your own mate started thinking it was better to have someone else choose for you, and those who had thought arranged marriages were better started thinking maybe it was better to choose your own.

"My head is squeezed," Keisuke said.

I thought a lot about my parents. If Grandma Fiorelli had arranged my mother's marriage, my mother would not be married to my father, and I wouldn't be alive, or if I were alive, I'd be different. And then I thought about Uncle Max and Aunt Sandy, and if Grandma Fiorelli had arranged Aunt Sandy's marriage, she probably would have chosen Uncle Max, or someone just like him.

I wondered what sort of person my parents might choose for me, if they were arranging my marriage. Would they choose someone like Guthrie?

Should someone be your enemy if/because he is your parents' enemy?

I said people should be allowed to choose their own enemies, and Mari said "What about loyalty? To your parents? Your country? You can't go around being friends with your parents' enemies—"

"Why not?" Guthrie asked.

"Because—because—your parents would get mad." Mari then said, "Wait a minute—that sounds dumb, doesn't it?"

I thought about how my father didn't like Grandma Fiorelli or any of my mother's brothers and sisters, including Aunt Sandy. It didn't seem right that they should be my enemies just because they were my father's enemies, and I wondered if my father was mad at me for living with Aunt Sandy and for wanting to know where Grandma Fiorelli lived.

What would you sacrifice for someone else?

This was a rowdy topic. We went crazy with this one. At first people said things like, "I guess I'd sacrifice my stereo if my friend wanted it," and "I'd sacrifice my allowance in order to save up for something I wanted." Then I said, "But what about food? Would you sacrifice food if someone else was hungry?" Keisuke wanted to know exactly how much food I was talking about.

"And what about a kidney, say? Would you sacrifice a kidney if your brother needed it?" Guthrie asked. And finally, "Would you sacrifice your life?"

On and on we went. At home sometimes, Aunt Sandy or Uncle Max would tap at my door and find me doodling. "Don't you have homework?" they'd ask.

"I'm doing it," I said. "I'm thinking." And I was. I was thinking, thinking, thinking all the time. At night sometimes I couldn't turn off the thinking, and on it would go, into my dreams.

. . . .

The Dreams of Domenica Santolina Doone

I was lying on the operating table and the Doctor said, "Dinnie? Did you say we could take one kidney or two? Can we take your leg also? And maybe an ear? A heart?"

"Who needs it?" I said.

"Crick."

I don't know what I gave to Crick, because I woke up.

. . . .

29

∾: Andermatt :∾

I almost didn't go to Andermatt that weekend, because we each had to have a ski partner who skied at our level, and I couldn't find any other beginners who wanted to go. But Guthrie said, "I'll ski with you, Dinnie."

"I can only do the baby slopes," I said. "I can't go up where you go."

"That's okay," he said. "I'll ski with you until you get tired, and then you can get warm in the hut while I ski with the others."

It was a small group: me, Guthrie, Belen, Keisuke, Mari, Fadi, and Signora Palermo. Then at the last minute, Lila decided to come.

"I really need to keep up with everything I learned at St. Moritz," she said. "Won't it be brilliant?"

I didn't really want Lila to come. I was having trouble getting used to this new version of Lila. Somehow the old complaining Lila was easier for me to deal with. Now, with all her smiling and hugging, with all her cheery, chirpy optimism, I was feeling a bit jealous. I wanted to say, "Hey, everybody, it's me, Dinnie, the same old friendly, nice person I've always been," but there was Lila, all sparkly and fluttery, eagerly grasping everyone's attention. The old Lila seemed to need me as her friend, but this new version seemed to be everybody's best friend.

We took the train up to Andermatt, looping and winding back up the spine of Switzerland, the reverse of the trip I'd taken with Uncle Max and Aunt Sandy back in August. Fat flakes of snow began falling midway through our journey. Around every bend was a more jagged mountain, a more startling scene of snow and chalets, and in the valleys cross-country skiers *swish-swish-swish*ed their way along.

Guthrie couldn't get enough of the views. He moved from one side of the train to the other. "*Guardate!*" he'd say. "See that valley? I bet it was formed by a glacier. See the steep sides of the cliffs, that U-shape?" Or, "Look at that one there! You can just see how torrents of water poured down forming those V-shapes, those steep sides!"

"Hey, Mr. Professor," Mari said to Guthrie. "Don't you ever relax?"

"Relax?" Guthrie said. "I *am* relaxed! This is me, relaxed! *Guardate!* Over there—look—avalanche barriers!" The barriers dotted the mountain slopes as far as you could see. "They keep the snow from crushing the town below," Guthrie said.

I was wearing the red scarf from Grandma Fiorelli, and I pulled it close around my neck. Avalanches. Crushed towns. I didn't like the sound of that.

And there, rounding a curve, was the vast Urseren Valley, with the town of Andermatt hugging the narrow streets at the bottom.

"The crossroads of the Alps!" Guthrie said. *"Magnifico!"*

Guthrie kept his promise and skied with me for nearly two hours on the lowest, gentlest slopes. He'd say, "Dinnie, you're doing great! You'll be up on the black runs in no time!"

It wasn't true. I wasn't doing great. I was still *downfelling* a lot, but it was good to hear him lie.

And I was ready to sit in the hut and sip hot chocolate at the end of the two hours. More than ready. Begging.

"I'll go on up and meet the others," Guthrie said. "I'll be back later. You okay?"

"Sure," I said. "At least I won't be falling in here."

An hour later, Belen and Keisuke floated in. "It's getting cold up there," Belen said. "Brrr."

"Where's Guthrie?" I asked. "Lila? The others?"

"Guthrie was skiing with Lila," Belen said, rolling her eyes. "Lila was showing off. She thinks she's a great skier, but she's not."

A little later, Mari and Fadi joined us. "Ooh, *raclette!*" Mari said. "I can't wait to get that big ball of cheese sitting in my stomach."

"Where's Guthrie?" I asked. "And Lila?"

Mari said, "Oh boy! They were having a huge fight up there!"

"What about?" Belen asked.

"Guthrie wanted to ski off *piste*, but Lila was scared."

A half hour later, Lila entered. She looked angry, but when Fadi asked her what was the matter, she said, "Nothing's the matter! Everything's brilliant."

"Where's Guthrie?" I asked.

She waved vaguely at the air. "Oh, up there somewhere," she said.

Signora Palermo entered. "Everyone accounted for?" she said. "Have you all eaten? I'm starving!"

"Guthrie's not here," I said. "He's still up there."

"Alone?" she said. "He's not supposed to be skiing alone. Who's his partner?"

We all looked at Lila.

"Where was he skiing?" Signora Palermo asked. "Who saw him last?"

Lila studied her hands, curled around a mug of hot chocolate. "I did," she said. "He's fine. Stubborn and fine. He's just *fantastico!*" A tear ran down her cheek and caught on her lip.

Signora Palermo grabbed her gloves and hat. "You all stay here. Don't leave this place." And off she went in search of Guthrie.

30

∻ Waiting ∽

As the blizzard raged outside, we huddled in the Andermatt hut waiting for Signora Palermo and Guthrie. Skiers poured in, seeking refuge, and each time the door banged open letting in blasts of raw wind, we looked up expectantly.

I fingered the fringe on my red scarf, sliding my fingers down each strand. I told myself that by the time I slid my fingers down each strand on both ends of the scarf, Guthrie would be back.

"Maybe I go up there, too," Keisuke said.

"Signora Palermo told us to wait here," Belen said. "She'll have a cow if she has to go out looking for you, too."

The avalanche-warning sign went on in the hut. Two of the top runs were now closed.

I'd finished with one end of my scarf and started on the second end.

Lila sniffed and pouted. "I told him to come

down," she said. "I told him not to ski off *piste*."

"I'm going out there," Keisuke said. "I'm not waiting—"

Belen pulled on his sleeve. "Don't go—"

Another gust of biting cold blew through the hut as the door opened, letting in a new batch of shivering skiers. *"Brr! Fa freddo!"* they said. "Can't see a thing!"

I was nearing the end of the fringe on my scarf. I was sliding my fingers down the strands very slowly.

Keisuke wrapped his scarf over his mouth and pulled his hat down over his forehead. "I'm going—"

Belen still clung to his sleeve. The wind howled around the outside of the hut, rattling the windows.

Again the door blew open and this time it was Guthrie who stomped in, knocking the ice off his boots and shaking snow from his hat. "Wow!" he said. "It's just unbelievably brilliant up there!"

"Where's Signora Palermo?" Belen asked.

"She's coming. She's right behind me—*ecco!*"

In she swept, laughing and shaking snow from her jacket.

"You're not even mad at him?" Lila asked.

Signora Palermo tried to look more serious. "Oh," she said. "*Si, si.* I told him not to do that again. You always ski with someone else, you hear me?" She stared at Guthrie.

"*Si!* I hear you!" He smiled his huge smile. "But you have to admit, that last run was *fantastico*, wasn't it? Such the best!"

I was so relieved to see him, I could hardly speak.

"You *loco* person," Belen said. She whacked him on the arm with her hat. "We thought you were dead."

"Me?" Guthrie said. "Never! *Sono potente!* Powerful!" He flexed his arms and sat down next to me. "Didn't mean to make anyone worry," he said. "I just couldn't come in. I had to keep going up that mountain and whizzing down. I found the greatest trail—some day I'll take you up there."

"Oh yeah," I said. "I ought to be ready for that in about twenty or thirty years." But I liked the thought. It would be me and Guthrie racing down the mountain, and I wouldn't be afraid, and I wouldn't be a dot.

Lila said nothing. She wouldn't look at Guthrie, and she trailed behind us as we trudged through the blowing snow to the train.

Most of us dozed on the way back to school. I clutched my lucky scarf. Lila sat off by herself, refusing to talk. Guthrie moved over to the seat beside her once, but she told him to get lost.

"Uh oh," he said, to no one in particular. "The pistol is back."

. . . .

The Dreams of Domenica Santolina Doone

My thin bubble was rolling, rolling, rolling down the mountain, bouncing through the snow. I had to keep wiping the mist from the inside. "Guthrie?" I called. "Guthrie?"

There was a loud crack of a gun, followed by a tremendous boom, and the earth shook and heaved, and then I woke up.

. . . .

31

⌒: Pot Roast and Plans :⌒

Aunt Grace and Aunt Tillie were at it again:

Dear Dinnie,

Tillie told me she never sent my Christmas letter to you. I'm gonna bean her someday.

Now I've got two bum knees. Why don't you come and live with me and help me out? I'll teach you how to make pot roast.

Love, love, love,
Your Aunt Grace

Dear Dinnie,

Your daddy is fine. We're cooking up a plan and if it works, I'll tell you about it. It's a doozy.

Crick finished basic training. He lived. He said he learned how to make his bed and iron his shirts and how to play poker. He's not flying any planes yet.

You will love our river if you ever come and see it.
Two thousand barrels of kisses,
Love from your Aunt Tillie, Champion
Cheesecake Jello Maker

32

~: The Pistol :~

The pistol was definitely back.

"I want to go home," Lila wailed. "And not to Saudi, where my parents are. They're going to be there for two *years*, Dinnie. Two *years*. I want to go back to the States. I want to live in a real house and go to a real school. Don't you want to do that Dinnie? Go back to your real house and go to a real school?"

I wasn't exactly sure what a real house was, or what a real school was either. Sometimes I got glimpses of places I used to live, but it wasn't houses I was longing for or remembering. It was the places around the houses: the air and the grass or fields or rivers or roads or barns. I remembered a dusty road in Tennessee and a tall crooked evergreen in Ohio. I remembered a hot-dog stand in Indiana and a park in Wisconsin.

Two of the items in my box of things, the box I'd been carting around for years from place to place, were tattered notebooks, one yellow and one blue, each with a picture on the front of a girl fishing. In the yellow notebook, I kept a record of my dreams. There were dreams in there all the way back to when I was seven. The first dream was this:

I dreamed I was a frog. I was yukky.

I didn't have very many dreams when I was seven, eight or nine—or if I had them, I didn't remember them when I woke up. But since then, I'd had loads of dreams, and there they were, all crammed into the yellow notebook.

In the blue notebook I had carefully written the addresses and phone numbers (usually we had a phone) of all the places I'd lived. I'd started the book when I was seven, and had to ask my mother to tell me about the places I'd lived before.

The first entry was Bybanks, Kentucky, where I was born, and the address there was just Morley Road, Bybanks. We didn't have a phone. I couldn't remember anything about Bybanks.

Then there were entries for Virginia and

North Carolina and Tennessee. There were entries for Ohio, Indiana, Wisconsin. And more for Oklahoma, Arkansas, Oregon, Texas, California, and, lastly, New Mexico. I hadn't yet entered anything for Switzerland. This was because I only listed a place as I was leaving it.

Sometimes I'd read through the whole list of towns: Bybanks, Dinwiddie, Swannanoa, Sweetwater, Euclid, Wabash, Antigo, Kingfisher, Calico Rock, Roseberg, Odessa, Chico, and Abiquiu. When I'd say each town's name, I'd get a flash of a picture in my head, a quick little image, one after the other, as if someone were rapidly flashing slides on a screen. I had a plan that some day I'd return to all these places, and there I'd find little pieces of Domenica Santolina Doone.

In my box of things was also the fold-up fishing rod that my father had given me. I could remember fishing in streams in Sweetwater and Kingfisher, in Calico Rock and Roseberg, on and on, me and my father fishing in streams.

I looked around at Montagnola and Lugano, and I wondered what I would remember about this place. I'd remember the mountains and the narrow Via Poporino and the lake. Maybe I'd remember the lizards and persimmons, shutters on windows, duvets hanging over windowsills to air.

"I want American water," Lila moaned. "Like they have in Florida," she said. "It tastes right. I'm the kind of person who has sensitive taste buds."

I remembered the taste of water in Oklahoma, with its faint smell of earth, and the cool, clear taste of water in Oregon. Would I remember the taste of Swiss water, with its pebbly smell?

"I want to go to a mall. I want tacos. I want hamburgers, real ones," Lila said.

I remembered throngs of kids in malls and a girl who got caught stealing nail polish. I remembered wandering around wondering where people got money to buy things, and what they would do with these things when they moved. I remembered tacos in New Mexico, fat, spicy ones that made your throat burn.

Would I always remember cappuccino and pizza *quattro stagione* from Federales in Lugano? Would I remember the rock-hard *biscotti*?

"Dinnie, don't you want to go *home?*" Lila said. *Where was that, exactly?* I wondered.

Lila didn't complain only to me. She bombarded Belen, Mari, just about everyone except Guthrie. One day Mari said to me, "I'd like to chop *her* up into hamburger and dump her in a taco. She's driving me crazy."

Two weeks later, Lila grabbed me as I left the dining hall. She waved a letter in front of my face. "Oh, it's too, too awful!" she said, and burst into loud sobs.

"What is?" I thought maybe someone had died.

"I can't believe they tell me this in a letter! I've got to call—make your uncle let me call, Dinnie, please—"

"What is it that's so awful? What happened?"

"My mother's going back to the States. She *hates* Saudi. Hates it!"

"Well, that's not *so* bad, is it?" I said.

She slapped my arm with the letter. "Dinnie! This means a divorce! I'm sure it does. But that's not the worst!" And she burst into loud sobbing again.

"What *is* the worst?" I asked, trying to imagine.

"The worst is that I have to go, too. I have to go back to the States with my mother."

I thought maybe I had missed some important development. "But Lila, I thought that's what you wanted to do—go back to the States and drink the water and eat hamburgers and stuff."

More sobs. "Not *now*," she said. "I have to go *now*. Next week! I'm the kind of person who needs some advance warning."

"But still, I thought you wanted—"

"Oh, Dinnie, you're always arguing with me. No one understands! No one listens to me!" and she raced down the hall, throwing her books aside as she ran.

Guthrie came around the corner. "What was all that about?" he asked. When I told him, he stared at me a minute and then said, "Well? Aren't you going to beg me to talk her out of it?"

"Oh. Sure. Talk her out of it."

"You don't sound very enthusiastic about that," Guthrie said.

"Well, doesn't it seem like she gets an awful

lot of attention throwing these tantrums?"

"Dinnie?" he said. "I never heard you say anything mean before."

I was embarrassed. "Was that mean? It was just an observation."

He zipped his jacket and took my arm, pulling me along. "One of the coolest things about you, Dinnie, is that you let everybody be the way they are. You're not always making judgements about people. But I don't know—this new observation thing of yours—I don't know—"

"Are you telling me I shouldn't make any observations?" I said.

"Is that what it sounded like, that I was telling you not to make any observations? *Non é vero!* Seems like a person *ought* to make some observations now and then."

I had a weird sensation, as if the wall of my bubble was so thin, that the outside was coming in and the inside was going out. It made me sort of woozy.

"I've got a great idea!" Guthrie said. "Let's all go to the Dolomites this weekend—there's a ski trip—probably the last one of the season. We can all go—you and me and Belen and Keisuke and Mari and Fadi and Lila, too. We'll make it a farewell party for Lila. What do you think? Isn't it a brilliant idea?"

"*Fantastico,*" I said. I didn't mean it, though. I was feeling very jealous of Lila.

"And this time," Guthrie said, "you're going to the top of the mountain!"

No, I'm not, I thought. I had yet to get to the top of a mountain, either skiing or hiking. Everyone else had been up to the top of the mountains in St. Moritz and Andermatt and even to the top of Mt. San Salvatore, right there in Lugano, but I hadn't. I was afraid to go, and up to that minute I hadn't been sure why. But as I stood there with Guthrie, I had an odd thought. If I got to the top, I'd be able to see over the other side, and what if there was nothing there?

As if he could read my mind, he pointed to the top of Mt. San Salvatore and said, "And the next weekend, I'm taking you up there. You won't believe it! You really won't! It's so so so *fantastico,* *meraviglioso,* and *splendido!*"

● ● ●

. . . .

The Dreams of Domenica Santolina Doone

I couldn't reach the wall of my bubble. It had stretched so far away. I was floating in the air near Mt. San Salvatore where the light at the top had turned into a candle and people were having a party and my bubble was going to bump into the candle and pop. It floated closer and closer to the candle, but I don't know if it popped, because I woke up.

. . . .

33

◡: The Visitor :◡

At ten o'clock that night, Lila, who was supposed to be in her dorm, banged on our door, demanding to see Uncle Max. She brushed past me and caught him sitting at the kitchen table eating pie with Aunt Sandy.

"This is mega-important," she said, "and don't tell me I've got to be in my dorm. I'm not going." Heavy sobbing followed.

In a thin voice, Aunt Sandy said, "Dinnie, I believe there's something we have to attend to urgently in the—downstairs—in—your room." Once she'd shut my door, Aunt Sandy said, "Grrr. Don't listen to me, Dinnie. I know she's your friend but she makes my blood boil over. I want to strangle her sometimes. I know she's got all those problems at home, but—"

"Problems?" I said. "You mean her mother moving back to the States?"

"That's the least of that girl's problems! That

family has more problems than a barrel full of—" She put her hand to her mouth. "Oops."

"What problems?" I said. "Tell me."

"I can't, Dinnie. I'm sorry. That wasn't supposed to come out."

"But what sort of problems?" I thought back over all the conversations I'd had with Lila, and I realized that she'd only ever complained about school. She'd never talked about her family, and I hadn't told her about mine, either. "Can't you tell me anything?" I asked Aunt Sandy.

"Dinnie, it wouldn't be right," she said, but she was wavering. I could tell by the sound of her voice, and the way she trailed off and munched on her lip, that she was debating whether to tell me or not.

"I wouldn't tell," I said. "I never tell anybody anything. Have you ever heard me repeat anything I hear in this house? Did I ever tell anybody about the affair Mr. Leyland was having or about the night Miss Fletcher came here drunk or when—"

She hugged me. "Dinnie, this house is like the set of a soap opera sometimes, isn't it? People barging in day and night to complain or weep or yell or demand—it's a zoo. You've been very good about ignoring all that, and I'm just sorry you have to hear it. If I were Max, I'd be a basket case. In fact, I *am* a basket case, and I don't have to deal with what he has to deal with!"

"So will you tell me about Lila?"

Aunt Sandy opened my door slightly and listened. Lila was shouting at Uncle Max. Aunt Sandy closed the door again and said, "Dinnie, I can't. If Lila wanted you to know her problems, she would have told you. Maybe she needs to have someone around who *doesn't* know her problems, who thinks she's a normal person with a normal family." She leaned close to me. "But then who knows what *normal* is, right? I sure don't, not anymore!"

Uncle Max tapped on my door. "I'm taking Lila back to the dorm," he said wearily. "Would you come along?" he asked Aunt Sandy.

"Be right there," Aunt Sandy said. To me, she said, "Dinnie, I tell you what. After Lila goes back to the States, then I'll tell you her problems, okay? But only if you keep them to yourself, okay?"

I lay on my bed and tried to imagine Lila's

problems. I thought of really, really horrible things. I imagined more and more, so that after a while, Lila was beginning to resemble a victim of every disaster we'd learned about in Global Awareness Month. I was regretting my observation to Guthrie about her tantrums, and I was glad he'd thought about the farewell party idea. I vowed that I'd be really really nice to her.

It's easier, though, to make such a vow than keep it.

34

∻ The Dolomites ∻

Signora Palermo and Mr. Bonner were our chaperones on the Dolomites trip. We left just before dawn in one of the school vans, in eerie blue-black light. Lugano's snow had melted, but Guthrie said he'd listened to the ski reports and the Dolomites had gotten twelve inches of new snow overnight.

Mr. Bonner made a great show of passing out transceivers, which the school had just acquired. They were yellow, and looked like small portable radios. You fastened them to your belt, Mr. Bonner said, "and then when an avalanche gets you and buries you, this sends out a little signal."

"Avalanche?" I said. "Are we expecting an avalanche?"

"No, no, no," Signora Palermo said. "Is protection, we try them!"

"So what exactly would a rescuer find?" Mari

asked. "A dead body? I mean if you're already dead, what's the point?"

"You can stay alive," Guthrie said, "even if you get buried. What you do is this—" and he went on to describe how you could create an air space around you, but I wasn't listening, because I'd wrapped my lucky red scarf around me and let the blue-black light and the rocking of the van put me to sleep.

. . . .

The Dreams of Domenica Santolina Doone

I was standing on a mountain aiming a transceiver at the sun. It made a little click-clicking sound. The sun sent back a bright, warm ray onto my forehead. I felt blessed.

. . . .

I think we went south from Lugano and crossed the Italian border at Chiasso. I remember little of the trip, just the rocking of the van, and occasionally waking to catch sight of a lake, a valley, a castle perched above a gorge. I caught odd fragments of people talking. Guthrie was telling Keisuke that *dolomites* were limestone rocks.

I heard Mr. Bonner say we'd be passing near Verona and Padua, where Romeo and Juliet had lived, and I heard him mention something about a thinking question and Belen said, "No thinking! No thinking allowed today!"

Lila, in her bright-pink ski jacket, huddled by herself in the seat in front of me. She seemed preoccupied, staring out the window, not talking to anyone. I felt I should talk with her, but I couldn't keep my eyes open, couldn't get my brain to think of anything to say. *Later*, I thought. *When I wake up, I'll talk to her and I'll be especially nice.*

We all tumbled out of the van at the ski resort, everyone groaning and stretching, untangling skis and poles, sorting out goggles and gloves, and fiddling with the bright-yellow transceivers.

"Calling Mars," Keisuke said, tapping his transceiver. "Calling Mars. Anyone there?"

After we'd gotten our passes, we gathered outside near the chair lift. "Okay!" Guthrie said. "Now listen, this is Lila's day!"

Lila pressed her lips together and tucked her chin into her jacket. She seemed embarrassed, but pleased. I saw Belen nudge Keisuke. I don't think Belen was too excited about it being Lila's day.

"And so I think we should all ski together, and Lila can lead, and we'll follow her anywhere she wants to go!" Guthrie said.

My heart started thump-thumping, but I couldn't speak. Fortunately, Mr. Bonner spoke for me. "Wait a minute," he said. "I can't ski all that well, and isn't Dinnie a beginner, too? Maybe Dinnie and I should stay on these lower slopes."

"Oh, come on," Guthrie urged. "It's not that much harder up there."

We all stared up the mountain. The first chair lift stopped about a quarter of the way up; the second one picked up beyond that and went up and up and up the mountain. It was very bright. All you could see was gleaming white, the whitest white there is, and the dark cables and chairs stringing up the side of the mountain, and the red and yellow and black jackets of skiers swishing down the mountain.

"At least ride up there," Guthrie insisted. "Ride to the top, and then if you don't think you can ski down, just get back on the chair lift and ride down. How about it?"

"Dinnie?" Mr. Bonner said. "What do you think?"

"Oh, Dinnie," Lila said. "Don't be such a chicken."

That pretty much did it. I did not like having Lila call me a chicken.

35

⌐: *Loud Snow* :~

s we rode up the first lift, I had to remind myself to breathe, because every instinct told me to stay rigid and not move, not breathe, just hold on tight. Mari, who was next to me on the lift, said, "Dinnie, the trick is to relax. Keep telling yourself, 'Relax. Relax. Breathe in. Breathe out.'"

Relax, I ordered my body. *Relax,* I ordered my brain. *Breathe,* I ordered. *Breathe in, breathe out. You're having an opportunity,* I reminded myself.

We got off the first lift and skied the short distance to where the second and higher lift began. At the second lift, Guthrie grabbed my arm. "Come on, ride with me," he said. He pulled me into line with him, and before I knew it, we were standing in place, waiting for the next chair. It scooped us up, and Guthrie swung the safety bar down over our heads.

"Here," he said, "I'll hold your poles. Just hang

on to the bar. Don't look down, just look up."

But to me it was scarier to look up, because all you saw was a steep wall of white. I wanted off, I wanted to jump, I wanted to escape.

"Are you scared, Dinnie?" Guthrie said. "Don't be scared! Look at this! Don't you feel so—so—*free* up here? It's like we're floating. And look at all that fresh powder! Such the best!"

He turned around to wave at Lila and Mari, who were behind us. "Hey, Lila!" he shouted. "Get ready to take us down the mountain!"

As we neared the top, I could see a short, narrow plateau on which to exit the lift, and then an immediate, steep drop-off of forty or fifty feet.

"I'm staying on," I said to Guthrie. "The only way I'd get down this mountain is on my butt."

He started to protest, but we'd reached the exit point. He flung the bar up, shoved my poles back into my hands, whipped the safety bar back down, and said, "We'll meet you down there— at the hut between the lifts!"

I turned and saw the others getting off the lift, staring at me, gesturing, obviously confused or surprised that I'd not gotten off. And then I saw that Mr. Bonner also stayed on the lift. He was three chairs behind me, following me down.

When I got off at the bottom, my legs were trembling. I was so mad at myself: mad that I hadn't gotten off at the top, mad that I hadn't followed the others, mad that I couldn't ski the way I could in my dreams. Mr. Bonner fell getting off the lift, and rolled to the side. "Oy, Dinnie!" he said. "I'm so glad you didn't get off up there. They think I'm coming to keep you company, but the truth is, I'm scared witless!"

We both stared down at the supposedly gentler slopes below, where the beginners were skiing. Even that looked steeper than anything I'd tried before.

"Tell you what, Dinnie," Mr. Bonner said. "I think we need some hot chocolate before we attempt that, don't you?"

We both managed to ski over to the hut without *downfelling* and were quite proud of ourselves. We took off our skis and stared up at the mountain, trying to spot the rest of our group. Lila's pink jacket made them easy to find. She was leading, and the others followed her single file.

"Why is she going way over there?" Mr. Bonner said.

Lila had swerved away from the other packs of skiers, and was leading our group way off to the right, where there was clean, untrammeled snow. As we watched, she turned to look back at the others and then lost her balance, falling and rolling in the snow. As the others came up behind her, she waved them on. Only Guthrie stopped and waited for her to get up and adjust her skis. She was waving farther off to the right, as if she wanted to ski over there, and Guthrie was pointing to where the others in our group had gone. It looked like he was trying to tell her that they should follow the others.

But Lila seemed to be set on going where she wanted, and she took off across the clean stretch of snow. Guthrie followed her, waving at her, apparently shouting something.

And then we heard it. It was an odd sound, a deep rumble, like muffled drums far off. There was a movement above Lila and Guthrie, subtle, shifting. At first I thought it was the light, the sun bouncing off the peak.

We saw Guthrie swoop below Lila and cut her off, grabbing at her jacket and waving his pole at the snow above. Lila swerved behind and then in front of him and veered sharply across the mountain, back toward the lift.

"*Guardate!*" someone near us shouted.

And then it looked as if the whole top of the mountain's snow came loose. With a thundering yet graceful slide, sending up clouds of lighter snow, a huge mass of snow broke free. As it tumbled, it pushed a wall of snow in front of it. It looked as if the whole mountain were going down over the gorge to our right.

My eyes were glued on Guthrie and Lila. I was tugging at my red scarf and praying aloud. *"Faster, hurry, move!"*

"Ohhh," Mr. Bonner wailed. "Ohhh, please—"

Lila was in front. They seemed as if they might be outside of the path of the avalanche, but as more snow rushed and gathered, it widened its path, surging behind them.

It all happened in a few minutes, probably,

but it seemed as if we were frozen there for hours, praying, staring, our brains unwilling to accept what our eyes were seeing. I could not move my eyes from Guthrie and Lila. I couldn't look anywhere else. I could tell from the yelling above that skiers were rushing down the mountain, aware of the avalanche on the far side, but I could only see Lila and Guthrie, the only two near enough to the path of the avalanche to be in immediate danger.

And then Lila went down, tripping, falling, rolling. Guthrie's speed had carried him just past her, but he swerved and stopped, and waited. It was those few seconds of stopping that caught them. The snow hurled down the mountain, spraying clouds of white all around, and they were covered and they were gone.

36

~: Signals :~

There was a brief deadly silence following the avalanche, when the absence of the rumble and thundering left a hollow emptiness, as if the roar of the falling snow had sucked all the noise from the air.

Later, Mr. Bonner told me that I was already shouting *Rescue! Help!* in both English and Italian and that I ordered Mr. Bonner to get help, and that even after the rest of our group, white-faced and stricken, joined us, I was still shouting *Rescue! Aiuto! Presto!* I don't remember shouting. All I remember is standing there like a stone, frozen to the spot, my eyes fastened on the place where Lila and Guthrie had gone down. I was feverishly fingering the ends of my scarf, as if it alone had the power to save them.

Almost instantly, a team of red-coated rescuers had assembled at the top, towing sleds and rescue equipment.

"Radio," Keisuke kept saying, "they have radios, yes? They have signals!"

"The transceivers, you mean?" Mari said. She reached down and touched her own, fastened to her belt. "Oh, blessed mother Mary, yes, they have the transceivers!"

Signora Palermo and Mr. Bonner were conferring with a policeman. Mr. Bonner was waving furiously toward the area where Lila and Guthrie had fallen. A rescuer appeared, carrying a walkie-talkie.

Still I could not move. I counted down the chair lift, fifteen chairs from the top. That was the left marker of the spot where they'd gone down. I eyed a clump of pines far off to the other side for the right marker. The top marker was the space of my hand held in the air, with the thumb touching the edge of the building at the mountaintop. The lower marker was me. If I drew lines from left to right and top to bottom, they would all intersect at the spot where Guthrie and Lila were buried beneath the snow.

And then I realized that the spot on which my eyes were fixed was where Guthrie had gone down. Lila had been behind him and off to the right. I tried to gauge her position.

The policeman and the man with the walkie-talkie were at my side. "Dinnie," Mr. Bonner said. "We have to show them where we think Guthrie and Lila went down. I thought I could do it, but it's such white space—it all looks the same—do you think you can tell from here?"

"They need to come down more, and over to the left," I said. I'd been through both ends of my scarf and started again. I was thinking *Come on, scarf, come on, scarf, do your magic.*

The man with the walkie-talkie spoke in Italian, directing the rescue team down and to the left. Immediately there was frantic movement up above. The rescuers were picking up a signal. The digging began.

As I stood there, I knew it was closer to where Lila had fallen than Guthrie, but I found myself praying it was Guthrie's spot, that I'd been mistaken, and they'd find Guthrie first, and then I was instantly ashamed. *Find her,* I wished, *and find her fast, and find Guthrie, and find them alive.*

I couldn't turn around, but I was aware that

Signora Palermo had gone off to the van to get the school's emergency number, and she was returning now and saying something urgently to each of our group. She reached me last. "Dinnie—"

"I can't look. Don't stand in front. I'm watching the spot—"

"Dinnie, are you wearing your transceiver?"

I tapped my belt. "Yes."

"Oh heavens above, spare us—" she said.

"What?" Mr. Bonner said. "What is it?"

She held up a transceiver. "This was in the van. Everyone else is wearing one. That means that either Guthrie or Lila left this behind—"

Belen was sobbing loudly.

Signora Palermo rushed to the policeman and guide. They asked me again to pinpoint where each skier had fallen. The guide communicated more directions through his walkie-talkie. "*A sinistra! Sopra!*" He told them that there might be only one transceiver, the one whose signals they had already picked up.

"Why don't they start digging in the second place?" I pleaded. "Tell them to start digging!"

"They can't just dig anywhere—"

"But I know where Guthrie is. I know it's him without the transceiver. Below, to the left. I know the spot."

"Dinnie," Mr. Bonner said, "the snow might have taken him twenty or thirty feet beyond where you last saw him. It's too wide an area—"

"Dig!" I shouted. "Tell them to dig!"

It seemed like an hour, but later they told me it was just ten minutes before we saw the pink of Lila's jacket and her body being placed on a stretcher and swept down the mountain to a waiting helicopter.

"Alive?" I shouted at the rescuer with the walkie-talkie. *"É viva?"*

He spoke into the transmitter, then listened. He spoke again, listened.

He raised a fist in the air. *"É viva!"*

Around us, shouts went up.

I kissed my scarf, but still I could not move. The rescuers were digging in a space below and to the left.

Signora Palermo returned with the news that Lila was unconscious, but alive. The rest of us by now were standing pressed up against each other.

Someone held my left hand, I don't remember who.

Mari said, "They're saying it's lucky it was early in the day. We have good light—"

Mr. Bonner said, "Dinnie, we've gotten through to your uncle Max. He and Sandy will be down as fast as they can get here."

I clung to these three things: that Lila was alive, that there was good light, and that Uncle Max and Aunt Sandy were coming. I felt as if they were three good omens, and maybe they meant that Guthrie would be found and he would be alive.

While I was standing on that spot of snow, I suddenly remembered the *voci bianche* in the St. Abbondio church on Christmas Eve. I thought about those white voices and this white snow, and I ached to hear the white voice of Guthrie.

37

~: Watching :~

Behind me, an Englishman said about Lila, "Lucky really. Caught in the side-surge instead of the full force. Awfully lucky." There were murmurs of agreement around him. "If she'd been caught in the full force, she would be buried beneath tons of snow. There would have been little chance of getting her out today, I'd say, and no chance of her being alive."

I heard Mari tell him, "There's still another one up there."

"Is that so?" said the Englishman. "I wouldn't like to be that person. No, I wouldn't like that at all."

Belen said, "How long can a person stay under there and still be alive?"

The Englishman said, "If you get them out within five minutes, that's very good—"

I didn't know how much time had passed,

but I knew it was more than five minutes, more than ten.

"—and up to twenty or twenty-five minutes, still a chance, but after that, not a lot of hope, I'd say."

Mari grabbed my arm. "Dinnie, it's been fifteen minutes. Fifteen!"

My eyes felt as if needles were sticking in them. I kept trying to picture Guthrie down there under the snow, and I wished I had heard all he had said about surviving an avalanche. Had he said you could make an air space? How could you do that if you were mashed under the weight of all that snow? Would your body heat melt some of the snow around you? Could you move?

Keisuke came up and laid his head on my shoulder. "Dinnie," he said in a shy voice, "this is *stew-pod*, this avalanche."

That was when I wanted to cry, when he said *stew-pod*.

While I was standing there staring at the spot where the rescuers were now digging, and while all my thoughts were on Guthrie, into my mind came an image of my parents, and then one of Crick and Stella and the baby. They didn't know I was here, they didn't know about Guthrie and Lila, they didn't know about avalanches. And then I got very frightened. If they didn't know about this, then I didn't know what was happening with them. What if one of them was in danger and I didn't even know it?

It seemed, right then, that there was danger all around, and I was afraid for everyone I knew. Oddly, though, the only person I wasn't afraid for was myself.

38

∴ Voci Bianche ∾

While I was trying to imagine if Guthrie could see anything down there under the snow, I remembered his story about the two prisoners looking out of the prison cell and one saw dirt and one saw sky. I wanted to know what Guthrie could see. There is dirt, I thought, and there is sky, and in between, there is the mountain and the snow.

I thought about Uncle Max and Aunt Sandy and Mrs. Stirling and the teachers, and how often they must worry about keeping us safe. I thought about my parents sending me on my opportunity and how worried they must have been, but how they wouldn't show it, and maybe this was because they didn't want to frighten me. They might be thinking all the time, *I hope she is safe, I hope she is safe*, but they wouldn't say it out loud.

I felt as if my whole family were down there

under the snow with Guthrie, and that only I could will them alive.

"*Guardate!*" There was shouting above and waving of arms and crackling through the walkie-talkie of the policeman next to us.

Mari crunched my hand so hard I felt as if all my fingers were breaking. Keisuke pressed his head into my arm. "I can't look," he said. "What they saying?"

The policeman threw his arms in the air.

"Found?" I said. "Found?"

He punched his fist back into the air. "*Si!*" he yelled. "*Si!*"

They'd found Guthrie. And at last I moved. I grabbed the policeman. "*È vivo?*" I begged.

There were more crackling voices; the policeman gave a *whoop* of air. "*Si!*" he shouted. "*È vivo!* Alive!"

I felt as if my bubble was bursting into the air and zinging off into the sky. "*È vivo!* Alive!" I shouted, waving my red scarf in the air.

The others picked up the shout. "*Vivo!* Alive!" We shouted and shouted. We grabbed strangers. We hugged them. We were a chorus of *voci bianche*: "*Vivo! Vivo! Vivo!*"

39

◦: Upstanding :◦

uthrie was loaded into the helicopter and swept off to the Milanese hospital where Lila had already been taken. A policeman accompanied Signora Palermo in a third helicopter. The rest of us returned to the base of the mountain and huddled with Mr. Bonner in the lodge, warming ourselves, holding on to each other in relief, and waiting for Uncle Max and Aunt Sandy.

They arrived just before dark, bursting into the lodge, staring wildly around and swooping down on us when I waved a tentative glove at them. I was very glad to see them; we all were. Calm Uncle Max. He would take over now, and we were glad to let him.

But he was flustered at first. After he learned that Guthrie and Lila had both been found and were both alive and in the Milanese hospital, he kept pressing his hand to his chest as if to keep his heart from leaping out of it. He hugged me and then went up and hugged everyone in our group. Aunt Sandy wrapped her arms around me and wouldn't let go. It felt good.

She kept saying, "Dinnie, you're okay? Everyone else is okay? You sure you're okay? Everybody's okay, right? Dinnie, you're okay?"

They wanted to know exactly what had happened, from start to finish, and so we told them, with each of us bursting in to add details. Then Uncle Max left for Milan, with Mr. Bonner following in the van with Belen, Keisuke, and Mari. I wanted to go with them, but Aunt Sandy asked me to stay behind with her to make calls to Lila's and Guthrie's parents and to finish a police report. We would spend the night in a nearby hotel; one of the rescuers had offered to take us on to Milan to meet Uncle Max the next day.

Aunt Sandy had trouble reaching Lila's and Guthrie's parents. When she finally did get through to Lila's father in Saudi Arabia, he yelled at her. She kept holding the phone out from her ear. I heard her say, "There *were* chaperones, sir," and "We don't have that information yet," and

"I'll give you the hospital number," and "We think you should come," and then, "Oh, I see."

When Aunt Sandy hung up the phone, she said, "I think I need a bourbon. That man is impossible! He's no pistol—he's a double-barreled shotgun!"

Apparently he was irate that his daughter had been "running loose all over the world," and he was furious that we didn't have an up-to-the-minute doctor's report, and he was doubly furious at his wife, who had apparently left for America that morning, and no, he could not come to Italy because he was in the middle of Important Business.

Aunt Sandy said, "And he added that we'd better see that nothing else happens to his daughter, and we'd better see that she gets the best care available, and we'd better contact her mother ourselves, and we'd better see that he gets hourly reports. I left out all the swearing, Dinnie. He sure can swear!"

It was worse trying to contact Guthrie's parents because we couldn't find them. When there was no answer at their home in Connecticut, Aunt

Sandy tried two other emergency numbers the school had given her. No answer on one, and on the second, an answering machine. Aunt Sandy left a message, and kept redialling the numbers every ten minutes.

Three hours later, she got through to Guthrie's aunt, who said that Guthrie's father was traveling. I heard Aunt Sandy say, "Somewhere in Canada? Any idea where in Canada?" and then, "What about his mother?" and then, "Oh. I see. I'm sorry. I didn't know."

She hung up the phone and said, "Did you know Guthrie doesn't have a mother?"

"What do you mean?" I said. "She died?"

"I don't know," Aunt Sandy said. "All his aunt said was, 'He doesn't have a mother.'"

We lay down beside each other on the bed, and I thought about the motherless Guthrie, and I wanted to rush to the hospital and ask him what had happened to his mother and tell him that I'd felt motherless, too. But I knew that his situation and mine were different, that Guthrie would never see his mother again, and mine was still alive, and I would see her again. Probably.

And then I thought about Lila's cursing father and her mother dashing off to the States, and I felt a sharp, sudden sympathy for Lila, and a flood of affection for my own parents with their zany style, their nomadic existence, and even their quirky forgetfulness.

Aunt Sandy said, "We've got to make a plan. We've got to think what to do next. We've got to imagine what Max would do." She held my hand. "Those poor kids," she said, "those poor, poor kids."

At our hotel in the Dolomites that night, we were either on the phone or waiting for it to ring. Just after midnight, Uncle Max phoned from the hospital in Milan. Lila was conscious. They were still running tests on her, but it appeared that she'd suffered only a broken arm. Uncle Max took it as a good sign that she had already complained about not having a private room in the hospital.

Reports on Guthrie's condition came in more slowly. It wasn't until nearly two in the morning that we learned he had broken his right leg in two places and had four broken ribs. Later we learned that he had to have stitches in both his right arm and his face for gashes from his ski poles. More worrying, though, was that he was still unconscious, all through the night.

We still hadn't been able to reach Guthrie's father or Lila's mother. Uncle Max said Lila's father had phoned the hospital and given him "an earful."

. . . .

The Dreams of Domenica Santolina Doone

The ski lift was open and crowded with skiers. I took the first lift up, skied over to the second lift, and scooted aboard.

I took in all the view, the smooth snow off to the left, the lumpier piles where the avalanche had crashed down far off to the right. I loosened my lucky red scarf and stared up the mountain and saw the sky, a deep, pure blue above.

At the top, I slipped off the chair lift without down-felling, and glanced down the other side. There was something there: more mountains. I slid over the lip of the plateau, and started down, letting my body move from left to right, right to left.

It was not like a dream. There was the sky above me and the white snow all around me, and I knew I could do this. I might downfell a few times, but then again, maybe I wouldn't. Maybe I would stay up. What would Keisuke call that? Upstanding?

I felt the air, cool and clean, coming in through my nose and filling up my whole self. I wanted to laugh. I wanted to lift off the earth and fly. I felt so—

"Sono libero!" *That's what I felt and that's what I shouted.* "Libero, libero, liberooooooo—" *It then occurred to me that since I was a girl maybe I had to say* Libera! *instead of* Libero! *but not being sure, I shouted both. I shouted for me and I shouted for Guthrie and for Lila.* "Libero! Libera! Libero! Liberaaaaa—"

Something was different. My bubble was gone.

By the time I got to the bottom, I understood exactly what Guthrie meant when he shouted Libero! *It was a celebration of being alive.*

· ·

40

∽: Two Pistols :∾

Early the next morning, when we learned that Guthrie was finally conscious and out of immediate danger, Aunt Sandy and I jumped on the bed and whooped and shouted: *He made it! He made it!* Then the phone rang again, and it was Lila's mother.

According to Aunt Sandy, Lila's mother said, "I've just gotten off a transatlantic flight and you want me to get back on another one?" She also added that she knew she shouldn't have let her daughter go to "that school." She had known her daughter would get into some sort of trouble.

Aunt Sandy said, "The avalanche wasn't Lila's fault." Then she held the phone away from her ear, while Lila's mother told Aunt Sandy that she didn't like her tone. In the end, Lila's mother said she'd be on the next flight to Milan, but that she expected the school to foot the bill.

When Aunt Sandy phoned Guthrie's father,

he said, "Is Petie okay?" Petie? I'd forgotten that Peter was Guthrie's first name, and I couldn't imagine anyone calling him Petie. Guthrie's father said he would come instantly.

When we got to Milan, Aunt Sandy and I were able to see Lila first. She was propped up in bed flipping through a magazine and scolding a nurse, who, with luck, couldn't understand her. "Honestly," she said. "Don't you have any American magazines? I can't read this!" But when she saw us, she instantly broke into sobs. "Oh, Dinnie! I almost died! Oh, Dinnie, Dinnie!"

The nurse rolled her eyes at us. Maybe she could understand English after all.

"There, there," Aunt Sandy soothed. "You'll be fine. You look great—"

"I do not!" Lila said. "Look at this arm!" She held out her cast. "It hurts! And look at my bruises!" She held out her other arm, revealing two fat round purple splotches. "And look here—" She pushed her hair back to reveal a small cut below her ear, a tiny rim of dark blood dried along its edge. "A gash!"

"But no stitches at least," Aunt Sandy said.

Lila ignored her. "And here, look at my knees!" She lifted her gown to show us her purplish bruised knees.

Aunt Sandy nudged me. She said, "Oh, Lila! That's terrible. You're a mess! What a trauma!"

"Yes," I agreed. "You look really awful."

She sniffed. "I'm the kind of person who is very sensitive to pain," she said, and then quickly, "Are my parents coming?"

Aunt Sandy said, "Your mother should be here tomorrow."

"And my father?" Lila said.

"I think he's detained on business," Aunt Sandy said.

"Oh, right," Lila said scornfully. "Detained. Business."

I was relieved when Uncle Max came in and suggested we visit Guthrie. As we left, Lila said to Uncle Max, "Can't you find me any American magazines?"

Same old Lila, I thought. Not even an avalanche was going to change her.

Guthrie truly did look terrible. He was lying on the bed with his eyes closed. His leg was in a cast and propped in the air; his face was pale and swollen and half-covered with a thick bandage, his chest was taped round, and his forearm was also covered in a bandage.

When I touched his hand, he opened his eyes. "Oh, hi, Dinnie!" he said. "Hi there," he said to Aunt Sandy. He sniffed my jacket. "You smell like real air!"

And at that instant, when he said "You smell like real air!" I understood his story about the two prisoners. Guthrie was like the one who only saw the sky, and Lila was like the one who only saw the dirt. I wondered where I fit in. Was I somewhere in the middle, seeing the in-between things?

"Are you okay?" Aunt Sandy asked.

"Oh, yeah," he said. "I'm fine." He reached up and touched his face tentatively. "Can you hand me that mirror?" He held it to his swollen face. "Hey! Look at this! I'm a balloon-head!"

He asked how Lila was. "I bet she was scared," he said soberly.

"Yes, I think she was," Aunt Sandy said. "And how about you? Were you scared?"

"Yes," he said. "I was." Later, he said that in

the middle of being scared, he thought about the rest of us and he could imagine us praying for him, and it made him feel better. "Then, in the middle of *that*," he said, "you know what I thought of? I thought of how Keisuke says *stew-pod*! It made me laugh. I had a little inside laugh down there under the snow."

The odd thing was that Keisuke *had* said *stew-pod* while we were waiting for Guthrie to be found, and it was as if they'd had extrasensory perception, Keisuke and Guthrie, as if Keisuke had beamed him a funny word to keep him going.

Uncle Max, Aunt Sandy, and I stayed overnight nearby, and met Mrs. King (Lila's mother) and Mr. Guthrie shortly after they arrived the next afternoon. Guthrie's father was not at all what I had expected. I had expected someone as exuberant as Guthrie, someone bounding and leaping, tall and muscular, but his father was a shy, frail man, soft-spoken and timid. I think I had also expected Guthrie's father to exude wealth, to be dressed in tailored clothes, to sport a gold watch, perhaps, but his father was dressed simply in a faded pair of khaki trousers and a pale, rumpled blue shirt. Guthrie's father spent the whole day and night seated beside his son, talking quietly to him. Sometimes from the hall, we could hear Guthrie laugh his booming laugh.

Lila's mother was something else entirely. We were in the lobby when she swept into the hospital wrapped in fur, patting her hair, and snapping her fingers at an orderly. "My luggage," she said. "Get my luggage, will you?" When the orderly didn't respond, she repeated her request, louder, and then said, to the air, "Doesn't anyone here speak English?"

We'd reached her by this time. Uncle Max introduced himself, and was about to introduce Aunt Sandy and me when Mrs. King said, "Could someone please see to my luggage? It's out there on the curb where anyone could walk off with it."

Uncle Max and I went out and hauled in three suitcases. She must have planned to stay awhile, I thought. When we returned, she ordered Uncle Max, "Take me to my daughter!"

There were many loud scenes coming from Lila's room throughout the afternoon. First there was screeching because Lila was not in a private room, and then there was shouting because apparently Lila's mother thought the nurses and doctors would understand her English better if she shouted it. Then there was shouting between Lila and her mother.

"I am not!" Lila screamed.

"You are! You're coming home with me as soon as we can get you out of this dump!"

"I'm not!"

"You are!"

Uncle Max and Aunt Sandy took turns going in to try and calm things, but neither of them lasted long in there. Uncle Max would come out, rubbing his forehead and saying, "Your turn," and then Aunt Sandy would go in, and pretty soon she'd be dashing out, wringing her hands and saying, "Your turn!"

When Mrs. King ordered Uncle Max and Aunt Sandy to get her "out of this dump" and find her a hotel and a decent restaurant, Aunt Sandy whispered to me, "If I kill her on the way and get put in jail, will you come and rescue me?"

When they'd gone, I went in to see Lila. Now she did look terrible, her eyes all puffed from crying, her face red and swollen, her hair in tangled knots. "Oh, Dinnie!" she cried. "Dinnie, don't let her take me away! I won't go. I won't!"

"Lila, maybe it will be better than you expect. Maybe it's an opportunity," I said.

"Opportunity!" she shrieked. "Oh, Dinnie, how can you say such a horrid thing? I hate you. I hate, hate, hate you!"

By the next morning, however, when she'd been subdued (I suspected the doctors might have given both her and her mother something to calm them, because they both seemed much more restrained), she loved, loved, loved me, and she loved, loved, loved Uncle Max and Aunt Sandy, and she loved, loved, loved Guthrie, and she loved, loved, loved the school, and she would never ever in a million years forget us. We were hugged and kissed, and then off they went, Lila and her mother, in a taxi full of luggage.

And that was it. The two pistols were gone.

41

~: Hats and Bugs :~

In the middle of April, Aunt Grace and Aunt Tillie sent Easter cards:

Dear Dinnie,

> *Happy Easter! Do they celebrate Easter there?*
>
> *I got a new hat. It's as pretty as anything. Too bad it has to go on an old head like mine.*
>
> *We had ham for Easter dinner. I wanted pot roast, but Lonnie says you have to have ham on Easter. I hate ham.*
>
> *Love, love, love,*
> *Your Aunt Grace*

Dear Dinnie,

> *You are going to be so surprised if this plan works out! Your daddy is coming tomorrow to talk it over. I can't spoil his surprise.*
>
> *Crick is in Air Force survival school. He gets tossed out in the woods and has to eat bugs and snakes*

and find his way back to base. I hope he makes it. Bugs aren't very tasty, if you ask me. Better than pot roast though. Ha. Ha.

I found a turtle by the river and met a girl who is uncovering a trail. You'd like her, I bet.

Two thousand barrels of kisses,

Love from your Aunt Tillie, Champion Cheesecake Jello Maker

In April, I also received a Valentine's Day card from my mother:

Dear Dinnie,

Oops! I forgot to mail this in February!

Beneath that, she'd drawn a blue heart (*blue?*) with a fish (*a fish?*) in the center of it.

42

∽ Fishing ∾

By the end of April, Lugano was transformed. Warm air and strong sun embraced us by day, and rain cleansed the city at night. In the Piazza della Reforma in the center of Lugano, the pigeons and tourists had returned in droves, the geraniums were already trailing from balcony window boxes, and the trees circling the lake had burst out in bright green leaves.

On campus, the persimmon and magnolia trees were in full bud, and scattered here and there were pockets of bright flowers. White umbrellas shaded the outdoor eating area, and students clustered about the lawns, textbooks lying open, their pages fluttering in the breeze. Up on the hillside near our house, grape vines crawled over latticed frames, and sweet smells drifted in through the windows.

On the last Saturday in April, a month before the end of term, Guthrie and I took a long-awaited excursion. He was off his crutches, only hobbling slightly, and the scar on his face had faded from red to pink. It was a two-part excursion we had planned. The first was his contribution to the day; the second was mine.

We took the bus down to Paradiso, on the fringes of Lugano, and bought tickets for the *funicolare*, the little train which crept up the side of Mt. San Salvatore. We squeezed inside with throngs of tourists and stared out the windows as the *funicolare* climbed, climbed, climbed. Trees and bushes and rocks lined the route to the top. It was hard to get a sense of what was around you, beyond you. I kept thinking of all the times I'd watched the *funicolare* from my window across the valley. I'd watched it inch up the mountain like a red lizard, occasionally disappearing from view behind trees and then reappearing again, slipping in and out of the trees.

On the bench across from us were five climbers, squeezed in a row, laughing and talking loudly in German. They were clad in sturdy climbing boots, thick woolen knee socks, corduroy knee breeches and green windbreakers. A yellow patch on each of their jackets identified them as members of a hiking group. When they heard Guthrie ask me something, one of the men said, "American, yah? I know someone in America. Chicago!"

The woman next to him nodded. "Hans Dolmahn, our cousin! Dolmahn—you ever come across him?"

Guthrie and I looked at each other. "Hm," Guthrie said. "Dolmahn, Dolmahn. It does ring a bell."

"No!" said the man. "You know him, you know Hans?"

Guthrie nudged me. "Dinnie? You've been to Chicago, right? You ever meet anybody named Dolmahn?"

"It's a big place, Chicago," I said.

"Big man," the woman said. "Big man, big beard."

This happened a lot, this sort of thing. Someone would find out you were from the States and then ask if you knew someone there, as if the States were a tiny little country and you'd be likely to know most everyone.

When we reached the end of the *funicolare* line, we tumbled out onto a platform sheltered among trees. It wasn't what I expected. You couldn't see anything beyond the trees.

"We have to go up there," Guthrie said, indicating a curved stone path which led further up the mountain, another five hundred feet. I could just make out a cross on a stone church at the top. Up the winding steps we climbed, circling round the peak, until there at the top was a wide flat plateau. In the center was the small church, and surrounding it were benches and a railing.

"Oh!" I gasped. "Oh!" For there, beyond the railing, all around you, was the most magnificent view. It was as if the whole wide world was spread out before you and you were standing up in the sky looking over it.

Three thousand feet up in the air, you could see the whole of blue Lake Lugano, and you could see beyond Lugano, across the Alpine foot-hills, and you could turn and see Italy and Lake Maggiore and the Lombardy Plains. An impossibly blue sky stretched over blue lakes and over row upon row of mountains—some green, some almost blue in the light, and some in the distance still snow-capped.

"See?" Guthrie said, stretching his arms wide, as if he were grasping the whole world in it. *"Fantastico! Sono potente! Sono libero!"*

I had an odd feeling, as if I were aware of being a speck on this mountain, a speck in this wide scene, my little dot self, but also, simultaneously, I felt a part of it and above it and very, very free, as if this were my world, mine. *Libero, libera.* I breathed in the air, and I thought: *This—this is me!*

I glanced at Guthrie. He was breathing it all in, his smile so wide. I thought about his father. Mr. Guthrie seemed a kind man, but not outgoing like his son, and I wondered where the son got his boundless enthusiasm from, where he had learned to rush headlong into every opportunity.

At the top of Mt. San Salvatore that day, we stood a long time at the railing, gazing out at the world, and then we went into the cool, dark church and climbed to its tower and out onto the ledge from which you could see even farther across the Lombardy Plains of Italy to the south. Campobasso might be down there somewhere, I thought. I would go to Campobasso someday and see where my Grandma Fiorelli walked when she was a girl.

We rode back down the *funicolare* and strolled through some of the smaller passageways that twist through the city of Lugano. There were open markets selling flowers and cheese and pizza and huge, fat, three-foot-long salamis which hung from the stalls. We ate slices of pizza as we walked along, and Guthrie said, "Really, Dinnie. You've got to admit it, this is such the best, don't you think?"

We took the bus back up the hill, past the school, and got off at the Collina d'Oro and walked down the Via Poporino to our house, where I got my fishing pole, and then we hiked up through Agra to the *percorso*. Through its winding paths we went until we came to the stream, and then we sat on the bank and I cast my line into the water.

"You don't use a hook?" Guthrie said. "No bait?"

"I'm not really fishing for fish," I said.

"Oh!" he said, wrapping me in a sudden hug. "You're a very interesting person, Domenica Doone."

Interesting? Had he said *interesting?*

"And you, Peter Lombardy Guthrie the Third,

are such the best." And, because it seemed that that needed some sort of follow-up, I kissed his such-the-best cheek.

That day, I fished for all of Switzerland, for every piece of it I had seen and everyone I had known there. I even fished for Lila. And then I fished for my father, my mother, for Crick and Stella and the baby. I fished for Grandma Fiorelli and Aunt Grace and Aunt Tillie.

When school finished at the end of May, I'd be going home.

. . . .

The Dreams of Domenica Santolina Doone

I was on a raft floating down a river. There were other rafts tied up to mine: Guthrie's and Lila's and Belen's and Mari's and Keisuke's. We all had huge nets that we waved in the air. I scooped up my whole family, one by one and dropped them on my raft.

I am a transparent eyeball! I shouted.

We were coming to a bend in the river, but I don't know what was around the bend because I woke up.

. . . .

43

❖ Forking Roads ❖

The final week of school was a blur. First came three days of exams, followed by our middle school graduation ceremony, and the next day the commencement ceremony for the older students, the seniors. There was a mix of excitement and sadness during this time: excitement at finishing exams and preparing to go home, and sadness at leaving our friends and Switzerland. My friends would be flung to all the corners of the globe. Some would return the following year to the school, and some would not, but I didn't know whether I'd be able to see any of them ever again.

A month earlier, Uncle Max and Aunt Sandy had given me a choice. It was a choice not entirely mine, I figured, because first I had to find out what my parents wanted me to do. Uncle Max and Aunt Sandy would give me a plane ticket to America, and I could either go on to school wherever my parents were, or I could spend the summer in America and then return to school in Switzerland in the fall. I hadn't been able to make that decision yet. All I knew at the time of our graduation ceremony was that I was going home, at least for the summer.

We middle-schoolers had been pretty rowdy during the final weeks, shouting, racing down halls and across campus, pulling pranks. It was as if we had bushels of tumbling emotions and energy to get rid of, and we dumped them out whenever and however we could. Uncle Max took this pretty well, reassuring Aunt Sandy that all middle-schoolers went through this. "They're doing us a favor," he told her. "It keeps us from getting all slobbery over them."

The teachers seemed tired. Mr. Koo said, "You beanheads are driving me crazy!" and Mr. Bonner told us, "I want you all to leave before you ruin an otherwise great year!" Before our English exam, he told each of us, "Don't worry. You'll do fine," and it seemed as if he wasn't just referring to our exams. It seemed as if he meant forever, in our whole lives.

It was tradition at the middle-school ceremony to have a banquet with teachers, students,
and their parents. I was surprised that most
parents came, and they came from all over the
world: from Japan and Korea and Spain and
Argentina and Norway and Saudi Arabia. My
parents weren't there, but I had Aunt Sandy and
Uncle Max.

It was also tradition at this banquet for the
headmaster and Mrs. Stirling to give speeches,
and for their speeches to be followed by speeches
from four students, elected beforehand by their
classmates. We'd elected Mari, Belen, Keisuke, and
Guthrie.

The tables were laid with white tablecloths,
the lights were dim, and candles were on each
table. The boys were dressed up in sport coats and
ties, and the girls in dresses. We looked nice, but
odd, I thought, as if we were playing grown-up.
We were acting differently, too, because of our
new clothes and the presence of so many parents.
We were a little stiff and overly polite.

"You look very nice."

"Thank you, so do you."

"I love your dress."

"Thank you. I like yours too."

Uncle Max began with a funny, gentle speech about Variety. He gave examples of how varied we all looked and spoke and acted (that was the funny part, because of the way he told it and the examples he chose), and how variety was the key to what was special about the school and how much he'd learned from it (that was the gentle part). He got a standing ovation when he finished.

Mrs. Stirling was there in her low-cut black dress, her pearls and her high red heels. Before she rose to speak, she reached down the front of her dress and pulled out a tube of lipstick which she opened and swept around her mouth. Mrs. Stirling gave a stern and rousing speech about how privileged we were and what we owed to the world and how we must give something back to it. We were her "army of goodwill ambassadors, marching out into the world." I felt as if we were all getting taller, there under the eyes of Uncle Max and Mrs. Stirling and all those parents. Parents were nodding away like crazy as she spoke, and she, too, got a standing ovation when she finished.

Mari was next. She spoke about fear, about how she'd been afraid when she'd arrived, afraid of being away from home and of meeting new people. She told how the fear had slipped away through the year, "slipped away silently and secretly," and how we mustn't be afraid to try new things. It was as if she'd crawled inside my head and seen what I'd thought and felt. When I looked around, I saw my classmates nodding, smiling, and realized she'd probably crawled inside all their heads, too.

Belen followed Mari, singing a Spanish song about friendship. I'd never known she had such a tremendous singing voice, low and resonant and confident. She filled up the whole room with her song. And Keisuke was the next speaker, saying that here he had learned that anything is *bloomable*, and he said he'd miss all his friends (Belen cried when he said that), and that we were all going to "flow away" the next day, "maybe never seeing us in one pot again."

The teachers seemed to be studying us throughout the evening, as if trying to memorize our faces, maybe remembering what we'd looked like and acted like when we'd arrived, and how we'd changed since, and what we might become. I was looking around at everyone and thinking these things, especially *What will become of us?* I wished I had a crystal ball and could look into it and see us all in ten years, in twenty, in thirty.

It was Guthrie's turn to speak. He began by reciting a poem by Robert Frost, the one about two roads forking in yellow woods. A traveler pauses at the fork and looks down each road, and then he chooses one because it seems less traveled, but really he isn't sure if it is or not. In any case, he knows that some day, "ages and ages hence," he'll say he stopped one day at a fork in the woods and he chose this road, and it made "all the difference."

Guthrie said he wasn't sure whether the traveler meant that the road *did* make all the difference, or whether he would just say it had. "One or two or three years ago," Guthrie said, "we each stood there in our own yellow woods, and we each chose the road to this particular school. Remember?"

I was remembering the hilltop New Mexico town and Stella having a baby and Aunt Sandy and Uncle Max "kidnapping" me. I could have resisted. I could have run away. Maybe I had made a choice, after all.

"That choice," Guthrie continued, "did make all the difference! I don't know if this was a harder road or a less-traveled one—sometimes I think it was too privileged a one—but it was the road we all took, and it's what brought us all here to meet each other."

I was thinking of Lila, thinking that she should be there with us, listening to Guthrie. I wondered how she'd feel.

"Look at us!" Guthrie said. "Here we are, back in the woods, facing more forking roads. Where are we all going? How will we all meet up together again? Dinnie here"—he waved at me — "is going back to America. Keisuke takes the road to Osaka. Belen to Barcelona. Mari to Rome." On and on he went, naming everyone in our class of forty students. "And me?" he said finally. "Me? I'm going to America, too." He stopped and looked at his father. "But maybe I'll be back. Maybe I will."

Guthrie said he didn't want us to go down all

those roads yet. He wanted us to pause for a moment, and go back to that place in the yellow woods, to the point at which we turned down this road, to this school. "It has made—and will make—all the difference, because we will continue to affect each other's lives. Maybe in ways we can't imagine, but there is something in the air of *these* yellow woods—these here in Switzerland, which we have run through and hiked through and skied through—that tells me we will take pieces of each other and of Switzerland with us wherever we go. We *will*! *Fantastico!*" As everyone applauded, someone—I think it was Keisuke—started the chant and soon the whole room had joined in: "*Viva! Viva! Viva!*"

44

⌐: Shifting Light :∾

After the banquet, the faculty made their way up the steep hill to Uncle Max's house. I was allowed to invite some of my friends, too. This was our last chance for casual celebration, because the next day's ceremony for the older students would be more formal and serious, after which people would quickly scatter to airports and trains to depart, many of them forever.

I felt as if time was pressing in on us, rumpling our clothes and our emotions. I found myself gripping arms too urgently, regretting that this was the end, and grieving that I might never see these people again. I thought about how we had traveled together and studied together and skied and hiked and worried together.

I knew something surprising about nearly every person in my grade, and about loads of older and younger students, too. As I stood there in our house that night, in the middle of the crowd, it seemed that the most surprising thing I knew was that for all our differences in nationality, in language, in culture, and in personality, we were all more alike than not. I was very proud of this observation; it made me feel grown-up. I made a mental note to write it down later, but when I looked at it the next morning it didn't seem as profound as it had that night.

Keisuke told me that he wished he could follow Belen down her road through the yellow woods, and I confessed that I wished I could follow Guthrie down his.

Mrs. Stirling plucked a strawberry from a bowl and said, "What's all this about *following?* You shouldn't be *following* anyone! We haven't been filling you full of all of this"—she swept her arm toward the balcony with its view of the mountains—"all of these *bloomabilities*—so that you might *follow.*"

Uncle Max leaned into the conversation. "We do need followers, though. It might be better to follow intelligently than to lead recklessly," he said.

Keisuke said, "Okay, then! Belen can follow *me!* Me, I'm going to steam down road, I'm going to——" Off he marched across the room, his arm thrust out, the leader of an invisible army.

Mrs. Stirling planted a firm lipstick print on my cheek and sailed on to another group. Uncle Max sipped his wine. "So you'd like to follow Guthrie? Did you mean that?"

"Oh, I don't know. I wouldn't mind *invisibly* tracking him—you know, a fly on the wall. "

"Mm," he said. "Well, he does have an interesting way of traveling, doesn't he?"

I thought about my mother and me and Crick and Stella, following my father from town to town, and I remembered the exciting parts about traveling with him. And then I looked at Uncle Max and Mrs. Stirling standing there, and I thought that they and my father and Guthrie all had that same thing in common: a way of traveling that made you keen to go along with them, to see the world the way they saw it.

The next morning, I awoke to the sound of rain flicking against my window and to the hum of

Uncle Max's voice. He was locked in the bathroom, rehearsing the citations he would be reading at the morning's graduation ceremony for the
seniors. On a hook behind my door hung my
skirt and blazer, and beneath it were my shoes,
newly polished, but not by me. This must have
been Uncle Max's doing. He loved to polish shoes,
especially when he was under stress. It eased his
mind, he said.

Aunt Sandy, still in her bathrobe and carrying
two dresses and a suit, paused in my doorway.
"Well, Dinnie, this is it. *Andiamo!* Let's go!" She
held out her clothes, like an offering. "Any prefer-
ence?" she asked. "Choose the thing that needs
least ironing, okay?"

She slumped at the foot of my bed and
rubbed my foot. "Oh, Dinnie! I know I should
say something wise and meaningful, what with
you leaving in just a few days' time, but my head
is full of stupid details—what to wear, what time
we have to be there, how to ease Max's nerves. I
can't bear to think of you leaving. I want to lock
you in the closet, to keep you here."

She pulled a card from her pocket. "This just

came," she said. She leaned over and kissed me and said, "Tomorrow we'll talk."

The card was from my mother, giving our yet-another-new address. She'd phoned two weeks earlier, and told me about the move. She was hoping my plane ticket hadn't been booked yet (it hadn't) so that I wouldn't end up in New Mexico, because they wouldn't be there. They were going back to Bybanks, Kentucky, where I was born, and where my aunts Tillie and Grace now lived. My father had grabbed the phone and said, "It's a great opportunity, Dinnie! Wait'll you see!"

As I lay in bed studying the card with our new address, the phone rang. "Want to bet it's Mrs. Stirling?" Aunt Sandy said. "Wondering if the marquee is firmly up and if the umbrellas are ready?"

Uncle Max, still in the bathroom, called out, "The umbrellas are ready!"

Answering the phone in her bedroom, Aunt Sandy said, "Yes, it is. Yes, they are. But maybe the rain will stop."

As if on cue, the sun exploded through the clouds. The bells of St. Abbondio pealed the

hour: nine o'clock. From my window I could
see the crown of the white marquee on the
campus below. Over the top of the trees was St.
Abbondio, the stone church with its slim clock
tower. I remembered walking down its path the
day I met Lila.

Thinking of Lila reminded me that Aunt
Sandy had not yet told me Lila's whole story,
about her family and their problems, although
I'd had a glimpse of some of those problems after
the avalanche. Maybe Lila would tell me herself
some day. Maybe there were good reasons why
Lila was Lila.

Beyond and below was Lake Lugano, perfectly
calm, perfectly silver, but with that odd, shifting
light that made it, a moment later, pewter-colored
and then blue-gray. And there was Mt. Bré off to
the left, no longer snow-capped, and off to the
right was Mt. San Salvatore, topped by its blink-
ing red light. Creeping up San Salvatore was the
funicolare, the little red lizard of a train. Up, up, up
it went, inching along, and I thought of Guthrie
and me traveling up the mountain and standing
on top of the world.

I turned to look up the path to Montagnola and saw Herman Hesse's house and thought of the cappuccinos I'd had up in the village with Lila and Guthrie and Keisuke and Belen and Mari, and how we had sometimes done our thinking homework sitting outside the café, as cats roamed in and out between our feet. On the red bench planted on the hillside between our house and Montagnola, I had listened to Lila's complaints and to Guthrie's stories.

At that moment, I loved Switzerland completely. I loved it with every piece of me, with every hair on my head and every eyelash and every cell. I felt as if this was my home, and I was no longer a stranger. Instead, I was like the snail who carts his home along with him on his back, from place to place. I thought about my fishing in the streams and wondered if I was carting not only my home along with me, but also my family, too. If that was the case, I could take Switzerland and Guthrie and Lila and Aunt Sandy and Uncle Max and Keisuke and Belen and Mari—all of them— with me when I left.

45

∴ Ciao ∼

The commencement ceremony for the seniors passed like a slow-motion film. I felt as if I were a stand-in, an extra, waiting for my turn to go on. I kept wanting to leap up and shout, "Wait! Stop! Unwind! Back to the beginning . . ." and by the beginning, I meant last September.

The rain had stopped, and a misty pale light spread over the campus. Each dark-suited boy escorted a white-dressed girl cradling a bouquet of pink roses in her arm. The grass, still damp, left wet slashes on their shoes as the graduating seniors marched into the marquee.

Guthrie took my hand and said, "Looks sort of like a mass wedding, doesn't it?"

The pairs nervously took their seats before the stage, on which sat Uncle Max, Mrs. Stirling, and the American Ambassador, who would give the commencement speech. In the audience were teachers and younger students, parents and grand-parents, bobbing up and down with cameras.

I kept thinking about those words *graduation* and *commencement,* which seemed to be used inter-changeably. *Graduation* seemed like the end of something, and *commencement* like the beginning. It seemed as if both words were needed, not just one or the other, because this *was* an end of some-thing, and the beginning of something else.

There was an opening prayer, followed by the ambassador's speech, and Uncle Max award-ing the diplomas, none of which I heard. What I heard were the rustles of dresses, the pealing of St. Abbondio's bells, birds in the persimmon trees outside the marquee.

We sang the American and Swiss national an-thems, Mrs. Stirling read a final prayer, the seniors filed out, gave one collective shout of joy, and headed for the luncheon on the terrace. We feasted on salmon, shrimp, turkey and roast beef, on sal-ads and strawberries, mangoes and avocados. The air swished with laughter and with shouts.

It seemed as if anything could happen, any-thing at all. The *bloomabilities* were endless.

And then, unseen and unannounced, time steamed through the crowd, wrenching people away to gather their suitcases, leap into taxis, and vanish amid shouts: *Good-bye, good-bye! Arrividerci! Write! I'll miss you! Ciao bella!* And on down the Collina d'Oro the shouts echoed, as the taxis pulled away.

I had ten short minutes with Guthrie and Belen and Keisuke and Mari. They were foolish, wasted minutes, in which we asked silly questions: *Do you have your passport? What time is your train, your plane?*

Guthrie hugged me, handed me a small package, kissed me smack on the lips, and said, "*Ciao bella!*" He leaped into the waiting taxi and shouted, "We'll have a reunion. All of us! Even Lila! You'll see!" As the taxi pulled away, I could hear him shout, "*Liberooo—*"

For a while, I sat on the bench near the driveway entrance, waving people off, and then there were no more taxis, there was no more noise. I wandered back across the campus. Already the tables were cleared. Only a few empty glasses sat here and there on the stone walls; programs

lay crumpled on the terrace. The grounds-
keeper sat on a bench, talking with two other
workmen.

"*Ciao*, Domenica!" they called.

The marquee flapped idly in the breeze as I
walked up the stone steps, past the dorm where
housekeepers were already flinging duvets across
the windowsills for airing.

"*Ciao*, Domenica!"

In a heap beside the door was a pile of used
textbooks, crumpled notes, and cast-off clothing.
On up the Via Poporino I went, amid bees sailing
lazily across the narrow lane. The bells of St.
Abbondio rang the hour: three o'clock.

Uncle Max and Aunt Sandy were not yet
home. They would still be with Mrs. Stirling and
the ambassador, in Casa Stirling. Our house was
cool and dark. I unwrapped Guthrie's package. It
was a book of drawings of the Ticino. I crawled
into bed with it. There was the lake, the mountains, the *funicolare*. There was Montagnola and
Lugano. There were the paths and rivers and
streams.

• • •

· ·

The Dreams of Domenica Santolina Doone

I was still in my skirt and blazer, but with skis on my feet. I was racing down the hill toward campus. Branches clipped my face as I sailed along without poles, my arms spread like an ungainly eagle. Over moguls, across the path, wildly I flew straight across the top of the marquee. I wondered where I would land.

· ·

Ring-ring. Ring-ring.

I woke up, saw my blazer hanging on the door, noticed that on my feet were socks, not skis, and stumbled to the phone. It was Guthrie.

"Hey, Dinnie, I've got an idea—"

There were long shadows in Via Poporino, and an eerie stillness.

"Where are you?" I asked. "What time is it?"

"Did I catch you napping?" he asked. "It's nine o'clock. I'm in Zurich."

"What? In Zurich? Now?"

"I missed my flight! No problem. Keisuke missed his, too. We're in a hotel near the train station. Why don't you meet us and we'll stay up all night and then you can go back to Lugano in the morning?"

"What, now?" The house was quiet. I figured Uncle Max and Aunt Sandy were still at school. "I don't have any money——"

"Ask your uncle——"

"Nobody's home. Nobody but me."

"Well, then," Guthrie said, "come C.O.D. Cash on Deliverino! Seriously, Dinnie, come collect! It'll be such the best!"

I thought about it. Even if I found some money and could make the nine-thirty train, I wouldn't get to Zurich until one or two in the morning. "Uncle Max would go ballistic," I said.

"Tell him it's a celebration of your maturity," Guthrie said.

Keisuke grabbed the phone. "I told him it was *stew-pod* idea. Girl should not be traveling late on train by herself."

Guthrie was at the phone again. "Okay, okay, I'm sorry, Dinnie. It's not a good idea."

I thanked him for the book. "It is *such* the best," I said.

"Dinnie? Aren't you going to miss me? Aren't you going to miss Switzerland? Dinnie?"

The phone went dead. As I stood there staring at it, it rang again.

"Dinnie? It's me again," Guthrie said. "You didn't give me your address. I need your address."

I gave it to him, and asked for his address, and then he said, "I'll see you again."

"*Fantastico!*" I said.

After I hung up, I wished I'd gotten the name of the hotel Guthrie and Keisuke were in. Maybe I could go. Wouldn't they be surprised? Would Uncle Max and Aunt Sandy let me? But no, there was no reason to go, except to see them one last time, and then there would be those good-byes all over again, and I'd have to get back on the train to Lugano alone, all alone on the fast mountain train.

I was feeling pitiful.

46

~: Next Life :~

Three days later, Uncle Max, Aunt Sandy and I boarded the Lugano train bound for Zurich. They were taking me to the airport for my flight to Washington, D. C., where my father would meet me and drive me home to Bybanks, Kentucky. It seemed odd to be going "home" to a place I couldn't remember, to a house I'd never lived in.

We traveled on up the spine of Switzerland, my face against the window. *"Guardate!"* I kept saying. There were waterfalls, stone churches, terraced vineyards. There were the castles of Bellinzona, the rising Alps beyond, clear rivers, and chalets blooming up out of the ground.

An hour outside of Lugano, we moved to the dining car, where I sat across from Uncle Max and Aunt Sandy at a table laid with a white tablecloth. We gazed out the window as the train rocked along. We ate clear broth and omelettes.

Aunt Sandy kept pulling things out of her purse and presenting them to me.

She handed me the train stub from my first train trip in Switzerland, when we'd traveled from Zurich down to Lugano. "You'll want to keep it," she said. "It'll bring back memories."

A little farther along, she passed me a photo of me and Uncle Max sitting in the Piazza della Reforma eating pizza. "You'll want to keep it," she said.

Next she passed me a folded piece of paper. It was one of my kidnapped signs. "That's the one that says turnip—or blockhead," she said. "You'll want to keep it."

Uncle Max laughed. "Maybe not," he said.

But I did want to keep it. I wanted to keep all of it.

With me was my box of things—my fishing rod, my book of dreams, my book of places I'd lived. On my last night in Lugano, I'd entered my Swiss address in the book of places. Added to the box were my lucky red scarf and faded ski passes and hiking maps and photos of me and Guthrie and Lila and Keisuke and Belen and Mari. Uncle

Max and Aunt Sandy had given me a new, small suitcase, too, in which were packed the few clothes which I hadn't yet outgrown.

I'd left one last sign on my window: CIAO, SVIZZERA: BELLA, BELLA SVIZZERA! I'd also left my spider plant blooming on the windowsill, sending off its own new shoots that floated in the air, and I'd left the skis in my closet. Aunt Sandy and Uncle Max had reminded me they were mine to keep, and that I could take them, but I couldn't do it. If I took them, it would mean I was never coming back. I didn't know how I was ever going to be able to make the decision over the summer, about whether to stay in Bybanks or return to Switzerland. I didn't know what I wanted to do, or what I should do. I hoped, though, that when the time came, I would know.

At the airport in Zurich, as we waited for my plane's departure, Uncle Max kept rushing off to the airport shops. He'd return with something each time, pressing it into my hand. "Here are some postcards with Swiss scenes on them," he said. "Send us one as soon as you get home." And "Here are some Swiss chocolates. Your mother will like them." And "Here's a wooden music box for Stella's baby."

And then I was waving them good-bye, and walking down the ramp, and I was sitting in my seat, and the plane was taking off, and I was sitting there looking out the window like a civilized person, not screaming my head off that we were going to die. I looked down on Switzerland, on the mountain peaks, and I wondered how Grandma Fiorelli felt when she left Italy all those many years ago. Maybe Grandma Fiorelli would come back to Switzerland with me some day, and we'd both go to Italy, to Campobasso, and we'd both feel right at home.

Soon I could no longer see Switzerland or any land at all. I was over the ocean, miles high, and I started thinking about Bybanks, wondering what it would look like and how it would smell and how it would feel to see my mother and father and Stella and the baby again, and how soon Crick might come home. Bybanks. What would I find in Bybanks? It would be an opportunity, I told myself. A new life.

• • •

The Dreams of Domenica Santolina Doone

I was flying over the mountains and over the ocean, dipping and gliding and looping and turning. I could feel the air on my wings and I could see Guthrie beside me, flying along. All around us were white eagles flying, flying, and the bells of St. Abbondio were running in our ears, and the eagles were all singing in one chorus: Viva! Viva! Viva!